JABARI CREED
WHEN A PLAYBOY MEETS HIS MATCH

DES' AMOR

CONTENTS

!Stop!	v
Synopsis	vii
Prologue	1
1. Jabari Creed	9
2. Cassie	16
3. Jabari	23
4. Cassie	33
5. Jabari	43
6. Cassie	52
7. Jabari	62
8. Cassie	73
9. Jabari	85
10. Cassie	93
11. Jabari	102
12. Cassie	112
13. Jabari	118
14. Cassie	123
15. Jabari	129
16. Cassie	136
17. Jabari	141
18. Cassie	147
19. Jabari	153
20. Cassie	159
21. Jabari	168
22. Cassie	175
23. Jabari	181
Epilogue	187
Special Thanks	193
Text Alerts	195
Des'amor Catalog	197

Copyright © 2025 by Des' Amor

All rights reserved.

No part of this publication may be reproduced, distributed, or transmitted in any form or by any means, including photocopying, recording, or other electronic or mechanical methods, without the prior written permission of the publisher, except as permitted by U.S. copyright law.
The story, all names, characters, and incidents portrayed in this production are fictitious. No identification with actual persons (living or deceased), places, buildings, and products are intended or should be inferred.

!STOP!

Be sure to read "The Brotherhood of The Drakos Mafia 1-3" before reading this book! Click the link below to read!

https://tr.ee/tRh02IZ81d

SYNOPSIS

Jabari is **UNHINGED**.
Cassie is **UNBOTHERED**.
In "The Brotherhood of the Drakos Mafia series", Jabari Creed was introduced as a smooth-talking bachelor living by the hit-it-and-quit-it mantra—until he met Cassie. Fierce, independent, and unimpressed by his charm, Cassie refuses to play into his games. But one night of passion changes everything, leaving Cassie consumed with guilt for betraying her fiancé.
Ghosting Jabari to focus on her daughter and her relationship, Cassie walks away, but Jabari isn't letting her go that easily. Her rejection only fuels his obsession, and he's willing to do anything to win her over.
Find out what happens "When A Playboy Meets His Match"!

PROLOGUE

Cassandra "Cassie" Taylor

People always told me I had a good heart.

"You're so sweet, Cassie. Too sweet for your own good," is what my grandma Annie used to say.

I never really understood what that meant until I found myself trapped in a relationship with the fucking devil himself... Danny Thomas. A man who chipped away at every piece of who I was, until there was nothing left but a shell of the person I used to be.

Hear me out though! Shit wasn't all bad in the beginning. Then again, that's what they never tell you about abusive relationships. They never start with fists or cruel words. Nah, they start with promises. Promises so sweet that you're willing to overlook the red flags staring your silly ass directly in the face.

I met Danny when I was just 18 years old. I was fresh out of high school and ready to spread my wings. My mom was an amazing mother who raised me alone after my dad walked out. However, she was extremely overbearing and monitored my every move. I hated that shit so bad! I counted down the days until I turned 18 so I could get away.

Anyways, Danny walked into the shoe store that I was working at, and I swear it was like love at first sight. We exchanged numbers and within a few weeks, he took my virginity. I know! I know! How the hell did I save something so sacred for 18 years just to give it to a nigga I met three weeks ago? Cuz I'm a dumb bitch that's how!

When I tell you the nigga had charm! He was 6 feet tall and weighed around 220 pounds. He was a sexy ass light skinned nigga who wore gold fangs in his mouth. Listen, Danny was finer than a bitch! His momma was white, and his daddy was black. His momma was also his dad's hoe and the highest paid one at that.

Danny was also paid. He had a plug that supplied him with some of the best weed and had a shit load of customers. With his looks, fat pockets, a smooth talking, he could get any girl he wanted. So, I was honored to be the one he wanted.

He had a way of speaking to you that pulled you in and made you feel like you were the only one who mattered. He could make you feel like you were walking on air... until he finally showed his true colors. He was fucking evil!

Before Danny, my life was normal. I was close to my mom, had a tight-knit group of friends, and a decent job. Genesis was my best friend. Hell, she was practically my sister. We shared everything, from our dreams to our heartbreaks, and she was always the first person I called when life threw me a curveball.

She warned me about Danny, of course. Everyone did actually. Especially my mom. My mom, Carla, was ever the optimist, warned me to take things slow. She said she'd seen men like Danny before. Men who were too smooth for their own good. Basically, she felt that he reminded her of my dad, which was NOT a good thing.

But I was young and naïve, and I didn't want to hear shit anyone had to say about my man. He was feeding me, lacing me in designer clothes, paying for all of my self-care stuff and the sex was amazing. I truly thought he loved me and that he would be my happily ever after.

Instead, he isolated me.

At first, it was subtle. He would say shit like my friends didn't respect my relationship or that my mom was too involved in my life. He would basically get jealous when I spent time with anyone but him. But he would spin the shit and just make it look like he wanted me to himself in a romantic way. He would say shit like...

"I just can't stand the thought of losing you. That shit drives me crazy. You are my everything Cassie."

In my young ass mind, I thought he was just in love. By the time I realized what was happening, it was too late. My friends had stopped calling and my mom grew distant. She was hurt by my sudden coldness and refusal to visit. But shit, I was too far gone, too blinded by the illusion of love to listen.

―――――

Danny didn't like Genesis. In fact, he hated her. He said she was too opinionated and nosy. He thought she was jealous of what we had, and slowly, he convinced me to distance myself from her as well. The calls became less frequent. The hangouts stopped altogether. Eventually, she just... disappeared from my life.

I didn't realize at the time that it wasn't her choice. Cairo, her brother, had warned her to stay away from me because he was planning to rob Danny. She couldn't risk telling me, not without putting herself in danger.

Looking back, I wish she had. Especially since at the time, it felt like another piece of my support system crumbled. I was alone, trapped in a web Danny had carefully spun around me. The nigga was meticulous about it too.

The first time Danny hit me, I was too shocked to react. We were arguing about something stupid. I promise I don't even remember! It was small as hell like I had left the light on in the kitchen, or I spoke in a tone that he didn't like. His hand moved so fast I didn't even see it coming.

One second, I was standing there, trying to explain myself, and the next, I was on the floor with my cheek stinging and my ears ringing. He had been drinking so he was irate, and I honestly had never seen him so angry.

He apologized, of course. I mean, the nigga even cried! But shit, that's how it always goes. He swore it would never happen again, and said he didn't know what came over him. And like a fool, I believed him.

But it DID happen again. And again.

Danny didn't just hurt me physically. That man tore me down mentally. He told me I was worthless, that no one else would ever want me. He made me feel like I needed him, like he was doing me a favor by staying with me. Over time, I stopped fighting back. It was easier to just go along with whatever he said, to avoid the rage that simmered beneath the surface of his charming facade.

I don't know how I survived those three years to be honest. Sometimes, I think it was Carlie who saved me, even before I knew she existed. Every time that I considered giving up or just killing myself, something inside of me forced me to fight.

The night I found out I was pregnant was the night everything changed. Danny was in one of his moods, accusing me of flirting with the cashier at the grocery store. I tried to reason with him, but it was like talking to a wall. The next thing I knew, he had me pinned against the wall with his hand around my throat. I thought I was going to die that night.

Instead, I woke up in the hospital. He had not only choked me unconscious, but he also blacked both of my eyes. And as if almost beating me to death wasn't enough, he also raped me. I was surprised he actually dropped me off at the hospital. When I finally came to, I was so sore that all I could do was cry.

The nurse was kind, and her voice was soft as she told me I was pregnant. My first reaction wasn't happy at all. It was fear. How could I bring a child into this world, knowing who the father was? He would really think I was his possession now! I would never get away from him.

But as I lay there, battered and bruised, I made a promise to myself and to the little life growing inside me. I was going to get out. I planned to call the police and ask for a restraining order. Then I would find a women's shelter far out and he would never find me. I had it all planned.

Then suddenly, it seemed like all of my prayers had finally been answered. The night before I was discharged from the hospital, I found out that Danny had been killed from a Facebook post. I cried so fucking hard! If I could've jumped up and did the Cupid Shuffle, I would have. It was over. For the first time in years, I was free.

To the outside world who were oblivious to his naturally evil soul, Danny's death came as a shock. According to the Facebook detectives, he was killed in a drug deal gone wrong. Mufuckas were saying that he was shot by someone he trusted. I honestly didn't care who did it. I wished I knew though so I could thank them!

But freedom came with its own set of new challenges. I had no job, no friends, no family to turn to. Danny had isolated me so completely that I didn't know where to start rebuilding my life. I was scared to even call my own mom. The one person who I knew would drop everything for me.

With the help of government assistance, I slowly pieced my life back together. I moved into a small apartment, took a job at a local boutique, and started preparing for the arrival of my daughter. Carlie was born on a rainy October night, and the moment I held her in my arms, I knew I'd do anything to protect her. She became my anchor, and my reason to keep going even when memories of the past threatened to pull me under.

―――

For a while, it was just the two of us. Life wasn't easy, but it was ours, and that was enough. I didn't reach back out to my mom until Carlie was about to turn 2 years old. I felt like I was cheating her at the opportunity of being a grandmother. She scolded me for a good three hours before we hugged and cried.

Now, I have to damn near call the police to get my daughter back from her. And Carlie's little traitor ass acts like the world is ending when I pick her up. Their relationship is adorable, but I won't lie and say I don't get jealous. I was so used to Carlie only wanting me and loving me that I didn't like sharing her love with anyone. Nonetheless, I was happy to have my mom back.

Genesis reached out about six years after Danny died. She apologized for disappearing, before explaining everything about Cairo and the robbery. At first, I was angry. Naw, fuck that, I was pissed actually that she hadn't warned me. Then, I was angry that she'd left me to face Danny alone. But as she sat there with tears streaming down her face, I realized she was just as much a victim of her brother's schemes as I was of Danny's abuse.

We rebuilt our friendship slowly, brick by brick. Genesis became my rock, and the person I could lean on when the weight of single motherhood felt too heavy to bear. She loved Carlie like she was her own, and for the first time in a long time, I felt like I had a support system.

And then came Sam.

Sam was nothing like Danny, or at least that's what I told myself at first. He wasn't violent. He didn't raise his hand to me or scream in my face. But his words cut just as deep. He had a way of making me feel small and made sure to remind me that I was lucky to have him.

He was a mama's boy, too, and I can't stand her old ugly ass. Her name is Samartha... yes, I said SAMARTHA! And trust me, the bitch ais as ugly as her fucking name! I swear to God she looks just like Ms. Pearly off of "Friday After Next". I'm talking thick ass mustache and always smells like a whole pack of cigarettes. She is old and bitter as hell. Sam's dad said fuck this shit and got out of dodge as soon as Sam graduated high school. I don't blame him one bit!

Everything his mother said was gospel, and I always came second to her. She was the queen of passive-aggressive comments and always found ways to remind me that I'd never be good enough for her son. Sam never defended me. He would always brush off her insults with a shrug.

"That's just how she is. Don't take it personally." was always his response.

Luckily for them both, I didn't give a fuck about her bitch ass opinion. I only stayed with him because it was easier than being alone. But deep down, I knew I deserved better. I knew I was beautiful, and Carlie only did my body good. She gave me shape that most bitches pay for. Sadly, Danny left me feeling so self-conscious about myself that I didn't know my worth anymore.

One night, after another argument with Sam that left me feeling small and broken, I found myself staring at my reflection in the bathroom mirror. The woman looking back at me was a shadow of who I used to be. My eyes, once bright with hope, were dull and tired. My shoulders sagged under the weight of years of pain and disappointment.

"This isn't who you are," I whispered to myself. "This isn't the life you want."

The realization hit me like a tidal wave. I'd spent so long letting other people dictate my life, but it was time to take back control. For Carlie. For me. I didn't know what the future held, but I knew one thing for certain: I was done living in fear. Done settling for less than I deserved.

I'm scared, yes. But I'm also hopeful. Because for the first time in years, I'm starting to remember who I am.

And I won't let anyone take that away from me again.

CHAPTER One

JABARI CREED

THE ANNOYING ASS ring of my phone scared the shit out of me, dragging me out of the best sleep I'd had in days. My arm fumbled for the phone on the nightstand, and I sighed as my fingers finally wrapped around it. With annoyance on my face, I brought it to my ear without even checking the screen.

"What?" I mumbled; voice thick with sleep.

"What?! Nigga that's all you've got to say? You over there acting like Sleeping Beauty and shit like you don't have a fucking job. What time you planning on gracing mufuckas with your presence, Jabari? It's almost one o'clock nigga!"

Kenzo's voice boomed through the line in annoyance and sarcasm.

I rubbed my hand down my face and sighed.

"My bad, bro, I had a long wild ass night." I said, swinging my legs over the edge of the bed.

Kenzo's laugh was dry

"Yeah, yeah, it's always some excuse with you. Let me guess... you were with Zeke streaming some silly ass game or chasing one of these broads." Kenzo accused.

I grinned mischievously.

"Man, ain't shit silly about my game. Stop hating cuz you fucking suck. And I can't help it that these fans love me." I replied playfully.

"Fans? You mean those two people in your comments hyping you up?" Kenzo replied sarcastically.

"Nah, I'm talking about the thousands of subscribers I've got on lock, Bitch! But you wouldn't know shit about that, Mr. All-Work-No-Play." I shot back before getting up and heading toward the bathroom.

"First off, I have plenty of fun hoe ass nigga. Second, get your ass up and get to work before I tell Mama you're slacking." He replied childishly.

I laughed, stepping into the bathroom.

"You a bitch dawg. You just mad that mama loves me more than you." I said jokingly.

"Shit she might, but you know she won't let you hear the end of it if I call her." Kenzo countered.

"Yeah, yeah. I'm up, man damn. I'll hit the spots and check in with you later." I said, reaching for my toothbrush.

"Good. Don't forget to talk to Darnell about that shipment. I don't want any surprises this time." Kenzo reminded me.

"Got it." I replied shortly.

"Later Bitch." Kenzo sang making me laugh.

"Bye man." I replied, hanging up.

I set my phone down on the counter with a huge smile on my face. It was moments like this that reminded me of how much I valued my brothers, even when they were nagging me like old ass men.

I turned on the water, letting it warm up as I grabbed my phone again and scrolled through my contacts. My thumb hovered over a familiar name before I pressed it. The line rang once, twice… then went straight to voicemail.

"Aight mufucka." I muttered under my breath with frustration curling in my chest.

The automated voice on the other end had become an all-too-familiar sound, but it still pissed me off every time. I stared at the screen for a moment as the urge to throw the phone against the wall crept into my mind. Instead, I smirked, shaking my head as I set it back on the counter.

"Aight! Today's the fucking day. You're gonna see me whether you want to or not." I muttered to myself, nodding.

I hopped in the shower, letting the hot water wash away the tension in my muscles. By the time I was dressed and ready to go, I felt like I had a fresh start. Pulling on a fitted black hoodie and some jeans, I grabbed my keys and headed out.

———

The smell of greasy fries hit me the second I pulled into the Wendy's drive-thru. My stomach growled in anticipation as I ordered a large number six with a strawberry lemonade. If you know, you know! I parked to eat because who the fuck wants to eat some cold fast food. Plus, them salty ass fries hit just right when they are nice and hot.

Once I finished, I crumpled the bag and tossed it into

the passenger seat before starting the car again. The trap houses weren't far, just a quick drive across town. I put on my game face and headed to get my late ass day started.

Pulling up to the first spot, I was greeted by a couple of the guys on my crew. Darnell was already outside, leaning against the porch with a cigarette between his fingers. Nigga was only 24 years old but acted like he was a 65-year-old man. I swear he reminded me of NBA YoungBoy so fuckin' bad.

"Bout time you showed up, Nigga." he said, smirking.

"Yeah, yeah. I'm here now, mufucka. What's the status?" I asked, stepping out of the car.

Darnell nodded toward the house.

"Everything's running smooth. Had a couple of new customers come through, but nothing crazy. The count's in the green like always. You know I stay on my shit." He bragged.

I let him have that because he was right about that. His count has never been off. Not even by a dollar. The little nigga was on his shit.

"That's what I like to hear. When's the next shipment coming in?" I said while glancing at the others who were milling around.

"Tomorrow night. 8PM." Darnell responded.

"Alright. Make sure we have enough space to store the shit this time. I don't want anything out in the open. If we need another spot, let me know so I can cop something." I instructed.

"You got it, boss." He simply replied.

I spent the next hour delegating tasks and making sure everyone was clear on their roles. The trap houses were running efficiently, but I knew better than to get comfortable. One slip-up and everything could fall apart. I'll be damned if I get jammed up for any of these niggas.

After stopping at the other spots and ensuring everything we up to par, I decided to go see my mama and Pops Sayid. Driving to the family house always felt nostalgic. It wasn't where I was born, but it was where I was raised and became who I am.

As I started at my city through my tinted windows, my mind wandered back to the day my life changed forever. I was nine years old, playing in the living room when the door burst open. The cops stormed in, yelling and waving their guns around. My dad, Jayson, didn't even try to fight back. He just stood there, his hands in the air, staring at me and Pilar like he was saying goodbye.

I didn't understand what was happening until I heard the gunshot.

Pilar shielded me that day, pulling me into her arms as tears streamed down her face. Our mom had died when I was two, so Dad was all we had left. Losing him felt like losing a piece of myself. He was my hero, and I wanted to be just like him growing up.

With no mom, dad or grandparents, I thought we would be shipped off to foster care, but luck was on our sides. Adara Drako saved us. She took us in, gave us a home, and treated us like her own. I owed her everything. She wasn't just a mother figure—she was my world. I would do anything for her including give my life for hers.

My dad, though... he was everything to me, man. He ran the Drakos' drug operation with precision, and even though I was young, I remembered how proud he was of his work. I followed in his footsteps, not because I wanted to, but because I felt like I had to. It was only right.

It wasn't all bad, though. The Drakos boys became my brothers, and Zeke... Zeke was my favorite. No Diddy. His goofy personality matched mine, and we bonded instantly. We streamed video games together, pulling all-nighters and cracking jokes like we didn't have a care in the world. He was the only one I could vent to without feeling judged.

Kenzo kept me grounded, and Adonis taught me discipline. They knew how quick tempered I was and made sure that I only acted when necessary. Xander was like the older brother who always had my back. He didn't give a fuck if I was right or wrong, he was swinging. But Zeke? He was my escape. Don't tell that hoe ass nigga I said that either.

The sound of my phone buzzing snapped me out of my thoughts. I glanced at the screen, half-hoping it was the call I'd been waiting for, but it wasn't. It was a chick that I let suck my dick from time to time named Shayla. I never fucked her because she's clingy as hell, yet she continues to stick around despite me telling her nothing will ever come from it.

Shaking my head, I ignored the call and placed my phone on my lap.

When I pulled up to the family house, I parked but didn't get out right away. Instead, I leaned back in my seat, scrolling through my phone. A text then came through and I damn near squealed like a bitch when I saw who it was from.

Best Coochie: *Would you leave me the hell alone Jabari! I'm going to report your crazy ass!*

It tickled me how she thought she could ignore me forever.

A smirk tugged at the corner of my lips as I started my car back up.

"Aight. Time to show her just how crazy a nigga really is." I muttered to myself as I pulled off.

Chapter Two

Cassie

The past couple of years had been a whirlwind, to say the least, but as I stood in my modest kitchen with the smell of lavender-scented candles floating through the air, I felt something I hadn't felt in a long time—contentment.

Life had been messy and unpredictable, but now, it felt like I was finally getting a grip. Genesis coming back into my life had been the glue I didn't realize I needed. Her strength reminded me to keep pushing forward, and though our reconnection had been bittersweet at times, I was grateful for the sisterly bond we had rebuilt.

Living on my own with Carlie was both a challenge and a blessing. At just eight years old, Carlie was my little firecracker. Her laughter filled the house, her artwork covered the fridge, and her spirit brightened my darkest days. Balancing work as an esthetician while saving to open my own spa wasn't easy, but every client I took and every penny I put aside brought me one step closer to my dream.

Carlie was my motivation; I wanted her to grow up seeing that her mom could create something out of nothing. She would see that no matter how hard things got for me, I never gave up. I always did my absolute best and she never saw me cry or bitch about the inevitable. I sucked that shit up and kept it pushing every time.

And then there was Sam.

"Mommy, do you like my princess dress?" Carlie twirled into the living room, her bright pink tutu bouncing with every step.

"Of course, baby. You are the most beautiful princess I have ever seen." I squealed, kneeling to fix the ribbon in her curly hair.

Carlie beamed, giving me a toothy grin before running off to show Sam her outfit. I straightened up, smoothing my sundress, and glanced toward the couch where Sam sat scrolling on his phone.

Fucking Sam.

"She's excited about tonight. Can't you tell?" I joked, hoping to catch his attention.

"Yeah, she's always excited." he replied without looking up.

I swallowed the sigh threatening to escape and turned my focus back to packing Carlie's downtime bag. I always took a bag with us whenever we would be gone from the house for a long period of time. It would have snacks, books, her iPad and coloring books and crayons. Tonight, we were having dinner at Sam's mom's house to discuss wedding plans. Or at least, that's what I hoped.

Engaged.

The word still felt foreign to me. Kinda like trying on a pair of shoes that didn't quite fit but were too pretty to return. Sam had proposed six months ago, and while I appreciated the gesture, the moment had been... underwhelming. To be quite honest, I had seen better proposals on TUBI movies.

It had happened on a random Tuesday. I was in sweatpants, folding laundry in the living room while Carlie napped in her room. Sam had come home from work with his mother trailing behind him as always. Samartha was an unavoidable force in our relationship, one I had learned to tolerate for Sam's sake. That day, she'd been unusually quiet, sitting on the armchair and watching me intently as I folded a pile of Carlie's tiny shirts.

"Cassie." Sam said suddenly before pulling a small velvet box from his pocket.

My heart skipped a beat, my hands freezing mid-fold.

"What's this?" I asked, glancing between him and the box.

"It's what you've been waiting for." he said with a smirk, dropping to one knee.

Something I had been waiting for... Not something that he'd been wanting to do for a while or even something he had been thinking about. The moment felt rushed, almost scripted, like he was checking something off a to-do list.

"Cassie, will you marry me?" he asked, holding out the ring.

It was a modest pear-shaped diamond, simple but elegant. Exactly what I did NOT want for my ring. We've discussed marriage and wedding stuff before and I specifically told him that I hated pear shaped rings. They reminded me of old people. I wanted a square diamond with a gold band.

My eyes darted to Samartha, who was grinning ear to

ear, and I couldn't help but feel pressured. This wasn't how I imagined it. No family, no friends, no romance at all. It was just me, Sam, and his mother. But still, I said yes. Because despite everything, I loved Sam, and I wanted to believe in us.

The memory left a bittersweet taste in my mouth as I zipped up Carlie's bag and turned to Sam.

"Are you ready to go?" I asked.

He nodded, finally putting his phone down. "Let's get this over with."

That wasn't exactly the enthusiasm I was hoping for, but I brushed it off. Tonight was about moving forward and planning our future. And even if Sam wasn't as excited as I was, I knew his mom would be more than willing to fill the gap.

―――

Samartha's house was a vision of suburban perfection. The neatly trimmed hedges, the freshly painted shutters, the perfectly placed wreath on the door all screamed "welcome," though I rarely felt that way when I stepped inside. Samartha greeted us with her usual over-the-top enthusiasm, pulling Carlie into a tight hug before ushering us into the dining room.

The table was set with fine China, and a bottle of champagne sat chilling in a silver bucket.

"To celebrate the happy couple!" Samartha announced, clapping her hands together.

I forced a smile, sitting down next to Sam while Carlie immediately pulled out her coloring book and crayons. My girl didn't fake the funk for no one.

"So, Cassie, have you thought about venues?" Samartha asked, her eyes lighting up with excitement.

"I've been looking into a few options. I was thinking something outdoors, maybe a garden or a beach." I began before pulling out my phone to show her some pictures I had saved.

Instead of grabbing my phone, she waved me off and chuckled.

"Oh, honey, outdoor weddings are so unpredictable. What if it rains? I was thinking the ballroom at the country club would be perfect. It's classy, and we can control the weather." She said with a laugh, already dismissing the fuck out of my idea.

"That's... nice." I said, my voice tight.

I glanced at Sam, hoping he'd chime in, but he was busy cutting into his steak, oblivious to the conversation.

"Sam, what do you think?" I asked, nudging him gently.

"About what?" He asked, not bothering to look up.

"The venue. Your mom thinks the country club is a good idea, but I was thinking something more personal." I reiterated.

"Whatever you want, Cassie. It's your day." he said dismissively, taking another bite of his food.

"Our day." I corrected, my frustration bubbling to the surface.

Sam glanced at me, then at his mom, who was now scrolling through her phone to show me pictures of the ballroom.

"You should listen to your mother-in-law-to-be. She knows best." Samartha said with a wink.

I wanted to scream. Instead, I plastered on a smile and

nodded along as Samartha laid out her grand vision for my wedding. By the time dinner was over, my head was pounding, and my patience was hanging by a thread. Sam's lack of interest and his mom's overbearing nature were a toxic combination, and I needed some fucking air and some weed.

"This is very kind of you, Samartha, but I'd like to plan this with Sam." I informed her.

Sam sighed, sitting up.

"I just don't see why we can't keep it simple. A courthouse wedding would be fine, wouldn't it?" He had the fucking nerve to ask.

"Sam, I don't want a courthouse wedding, And I don't want your mom planning everything, either." I said firmly.

Sam rolled his eyes, muttering something under his breath, and Samartha gasped, offended.

"Cassie, I'm just trying to help. You don't have to be so ungrateful." She snapped.

Ungrateful. That word hit a nerve. I stood knowing that if I didn't leave, I would fuck some shit up.

"You know what? I think I'm going to head home." I said before standing and grabbing Carlie's bag.

"Already? You can't leave before dessert!" Samartha protested.

"I'm sorry, but I'm exhausted. It's been a long day." I said, forcing yet another smile.

Sam barely looked up as I grabbed Carlie by the hand and headed for the door. The nigga didn't even offer to walk us to the car. I was so happy we decided to drive separately.

The drive home was quiet, aside from the soft hum of *Sade* coming though the radio. I replayed the night in my head, getting more frustrated by the second. I couldn't wait to get in the house so I could call Genesis. She is going to have a nice laugh.

By the time I pulled into my driveway, I was ready to collapse.

"Come on, baby girl." I said as I reached back and unbuckled Carlie's seatbelt.

She was half-asleep, her head resting on my shoulder as I carried her big ass inside. She was small for her age, but she was a chunky something. She looked like she would be shaped just like me. Short and bottom heavy. I was only 5'4 and weighed around 145.

As I pushed open the front door, I froze. The lights were on, and I knew for sure that I had turned them off before we left. There was also a faint smell of vanilla and roses. A scent that I never ever use. I set Carlie down on the couch and walked further into the house with my heart pounding.

"Hello?" I called out, but there was no response.

And then I saw it.

A trail of rose petals leading from the living room to the hallway. My pulse quickened as I followed it, unsure of what to expect. When I reached the end of the trail, I opened the door to my bedroom and gasped.

"I KNOW YOU FUCKING LYING!" I yelled.

How the fuck did he get in my house?!

CHAPTER Three

Jabari

Finding Cassie wasn't hard. It never is when you know what you're doing, and I've been doing this a long time. Genesis didn't give me her address, but I didn't need her to. Cassie could run, hide, or disappear if she wanted to, but it wouldn't make a difference. I'd always find her.

And if I couldn't, then Zeke could.

Still, I hadn't expected to feel relaxed when I stepped into her cozy ass crib. It smelled like her. A soothing ass lavender scent that made you wanna go to sleep. For a second, I was taken back to that weekend we'd shared after Kenzo and Genesis' wedding. A weekend that neither of us had spoken about since.

Snapping out of it, I got to work. I didn't come here to reminisce. Plus, I had Cassie's location on my phone so I knew she would be here within the next hour. Like I said, she wasn't hard to find at all. I was just being courteous.

I began placing my small cameras all over this bitch. The cameras had audio too so I could hear and see everything. I put a camera in the living room, dining room, kitchen, hallways, garage, laundry room, Cassie's bedroom and her bathroom. Hell, I even put cameras outside her house. The only place I didn't place one is Carlie's room and bathroom. That's weird.

After making sure the cameras were in place, I began setting the ambiance. I began dropping rose petals near Cassie's bedroom and I lit some vanilla candles I bought from Bath and Body Works. I found out through Zeke that Cassie's new boyfriend was allergic to vanilla. I hope his ass dies.

After everything was set up, I went to sit on Cassie's bed and wait for the magic to happen. The opening of the front door brought me back to the present. I listened as Cassie stepped inside, and smirked when I heard her call out for someone. I loved that she was on point and knew something was off. Let's me know that she ain't no ditzy ass broad.

I sat the roses that I purchased for her and my lil homie Carlie on her bed and waited for her scary ass to finally come to me. When she walked into her bedroom, her expression froze the moment she saw me, morphing from surprise to fear, and finally settling on anger.

"I KNOW YOU FUCKING LYING!" She yelled, making me frown.

She had me fucked up.

"Aye chill with all that yelling and come give Daddy a kiss. Acting like you ain't happy to see a nigga and shit. I bet that lil coochie thumping right now with yo lil phony ass." I said while smirking at her fine ass.

"Jabari." She mumbled as she collected herself.

"What the hell are you doing in my house?" She added.

I leaned against the wall with my arms crossed as I got a good look at her. I tried my best to keep my face calm even though my heart was doing some weird shit at the sight of her. She looked fucking good. Nah fuck that! She looked fucking edible.

Her hair was pulled back into a messy bun, and her skin glowed like she'd just stepped off the cover of some magazine. She was wearing a sundress and the thought of her not wearing any draws underneath had me bricking up. Damn, I need some pussy.

"You look good Mama." I said smoothly, ignoring her question.

Her eyes narrowed.

"How did you find me?" She asked.

"You have to be lost for a mufucka to have to find you. I always knew where you were. I was just waiting for you to get yo damn mind right. Come on man. You should know by now there's nothing I can't find out." I replied, smirking.

Her jaw clenched and her eyes bucked as if she had figured it all out.

"Genesis told you, didn't she? That's the only way you could've..."

"Genesis didn't tell me a damn thing. I keep telling you that you were never low. You could move to the ends of the earth, and I'd still find yo ass. Be happy it took me this long to pop up on yo sneaky ass." I cut her off.

Her lips parted, and suddenly a look of unease flashed across her face.

"You can't just show up here! Especially uninvited. I

have a life, Jabari. You don't get to just pop up on some stalker shit!" Cassie snapped with her arms flailing all over the place.

The shit was actually comical until I noticed it... the small sparkle on her left hand. A ring. A tiny ass ring, but nonetheless a fucking engagement ring.

"You got me so fucked up!" I said, pushing off the wall and stepping closer.

She backed up instinctively, her eyes darting to the hallway to see if Carlie had awakened.

"Who the fuck gave you that ring, Cassandra?" I asked angrily.

Her mouth opened and closed like she was searching for words, but nothing came out. That silence told me everything I needed to know.

"You're engaged?" I hissed, keeping my voice low.

She nodded slowly causing an aching pain in my chest.

"To who?" I asked.

"Sam... he's my boyfr... he's my fiancé." she whispered, her gaze darting toward the hallway as if she was planning to run.

Sam. He don't even sound like a real nigga. He sounds like a lame ass bitch. Can't no mufucka named Sam handle Cassie.

"You're joking, right? You just tryna make me mad. That's it. Ain't no fucking way you getting married. Nah." I laughed bitterly, running a hand down my face.

"Jabari..." She tried saying, but I put my hand up to silence her disloyal ass.

"That weekend... You telling me that weekend didn't mean shit to you?" I said as I began stepping closer to her.

Eventually, I was close enough where I could feel her tension radiating off her.

Cassie's cheeks flushed, and I could see the guilt flicker across her face. She knew exactly what I was talking about.

"Don't. Please, don't bring that up." she whispered, her voice trembling.

"Nah, fuck that, I'm bringing it up. Because I can't stop thinking about it. About you. About how good you felt. How you tasted... the shit we shared. The face you made when I..."

"Stop!" She snapped, but it was more of a hiss.

She started wringing her hands and biting her bottom lip nervously.

"That was a mistake, Jabari. It shouldn't have happened." Cassie began saying.

"A mistake?" I echoed in disbelief.

I had to chuckle to calm myself down. I was seconds away from putting her funky ass in a headlock.

"Is that what you tell yourself to sleep at night? Because I remember you saying something very different at the time." I said.

She leaned back until her back rested on the wall behind her, and for a moment, she looked like she might cry. But before either of us could say another word, a small, sleepy voice broke the tension.

"Jabbie?"

We both froze, turning toward the hallway. Carlie stood there, rubbing her eyes and clutching a stuffed animal. The moment she saw me, her face lit up.

"Hey Jabbie!" she squealed, running toward me with her arms outstretched.

The pressure between Cassie and me melted away as I

scooped her up, holding her close. When I first met Carlie, she immediately told me that she would call me Jabbie because it was cuter than Jabari or Bari. I let her live cuz she's cute as hell and a sweet little girl.

"Hey, princess, what are you doing awake?" I said softly.

"I heard you and Mommy talking. You're here!" she said innocently, resting her head on my shoulder.

Cassie watched us, her arms crossed, but her expression softened as she saw how Carlie clung to me.

"Yes, I'm here, but I'm about to head out." I informed her.

Her eyes lit up.

"Wait! You have to see my room! Come see my room!" She sang.

She tapped my arms to put her down. As soon as her feet hit the floor, she grabbed my hand and tugged me down the hallway, leaving Cassie to follow behind. When we got to her room, Carlie pulled out her Barbie dolls and insisted I sit on the floor with her.

"Here. This one is you." she said, handing me a doll with long blonde hair.

I chuckled, glancing back at Cassie, who was leaning against the doorframe with her arms crossed.

"You hear that, Cass? I'm a Barbie now." I said, trying to get rid of the elephant in the room.

Cassie rolled her eyes, but I saw the glimpse of a smile on her lips.

For a few minutes, I let Carlie direct our little Barbie play session, doing my best to keep up with her wild imagination. Luckily for me, I've had a lot of practice playing with dolls from my niece Zahra. It was easy to forget everything else when I was with her. Kids had a way of making the world feel simple, even if just for a moment.

Eventually, Cassie cleared her throat.

"Alright, Carlie, it's time for Uncle Jabari to go."

"It's Jabbie." Both Carlie and I said simultaneously making Cassie roll her eyes.

I hope them bitches get stuck one day. Then she won't be so fine. I'll still fuck though.

"Jabbie, Jabari, whatever. Say goodbye so you can get ready for bed." Cassie snapped.

Carlie pouted, but I stood up, ruffling her curls.

"Don't worry, princess. I'll see you again soon." I assured her.

"Promise?" she asked, holding up her pinky.

I crouched down and linked my pinky with hers.

"I promise." I replied sincerely.

Before I left, I grabbed the bouquet of roses I'd brought for them from Cassie's bed. But instead of handing them to her, I knelt down and gave them to Carlie.

"These are for you," I said with a wink.

Her face lit up, and she hugged the flowers to her chest.

"Thank you, Jabbie!" She yelled in excitement.

Cassie's eyes followed me as I walked to the door. The expression on her face was unreadable. I didn't care to ask any questions though. I didn't even say goodbye. I didn't need to. She knew she had me fucked up. I hoped she knew this wasn't the last she'd see of me either.

As I got into my car, I had to throw my head against my headrest. Sam. I bet that shit was short for Samuel or some other gay ass shit. The thought of him touching her, or her touching him, made my blood boil. She didn't belong with him. She didn't belong with anyone but…

I shook my head, gripping the steering wheel tightly. This wasn't about wanting her for myself. Well, not entirely. I just couldn't stand the thought of someone else having her, of someone else making her happy.

Flashbacks of how she looked tonight had my shit harder than dried cement. I should've had her put Carlie to sleep and made her take this dick. It's cool though. I want her, and I always get what I want. I knew better than to rush the shit.

In due time.

For now, I'd deal with Sam. He didn't know it yet, but his days in Cassie's life were numbered.

I picked up my phone and called my right hand, Zeke.

"Yerrrr!" He yelled once he finally answered.

"Aye Bitch, activate them cameras for me. Shorty got me fucked up." I barked making him laugh like the goofy mufucka he is.

"Damn! Aight, say less. You'll be set in about 5 minutes." He replied.

"Make it 3." I said before hanging up.

I know he was at home cursing me the fuck out, but I don't give a fuck. This is imperative! I sat there for a few minutes and just as I was about to call his ass back, I received a text.

Zeke: *Don't hang up on me no more you sassy ass bitch. It's done tho. She gone beat yo ass when she finds out*

I didn't even bother responding to that dumb shit. I hurriedly went to the app and smiled victoriously as I watched her pace in her bedroom on the phone. I turned the audio on and laughed when I heard Sam's voice on her phone. This wanch thinks I'm playing with her!

I parked my car a few blocks away and hopped out on pure bullshit. I jogged back to her place and pulled up the cameras to see where she was inside. When I saw her getting ready for a shower, I knew it was go time. I almost stalled when I saw her getting undressed, but I shook that shit off. I'll watch the video later.

The second she stepped into the shower, I used my key quietly crept into the house. I knew I had to move quickly because according to her conversation, Sam's lame ass was on the way. I didn't have to worry about Carlie catching me because she put her down for bed and that little girl doesn't play about her sleep.

I crept into Cassie's bedroom and my dick hardened when I heard the shower going. It took everything in me not burst in there and join her ass. I could picture the water gliding down them thick ass thighs and... hold on! I don't have to picture shit! I got a camera in that mufucka too!

I hurriedly slipped into the closet and waited until it was time to fuck a nigga up. Her lil funky ass took two fucking hours in the damn shower. My fucking legs hurt from standing in this bitch. She could've at least had a wide closet where a nigga could sit down.

She finally came out the bathroom and I had to bite my damn tongue to stop from moaning out loud. She walked out that bitch booty butt ass naked! Her fat ass bounced without her even trying! When she grabbed her lotion and sat on the bed with them legs wide open, I knew I couldn't hold my nut if I tried. I whipped my shit out and started beating my meat. I could see her fat ass pussy peeking from between her thighs and all I wanted to do was taste it.

"Fuck!" I whispered.

Shortly after, I snatched one of Sam's hoodies from her hamper and nutted all over that mufucka.

"Ahhhh!" I moaned as low as I possibly could.

I hadn't had no pussy in a few weeks, so I was backed up. That nut took all my fucking energy. I leaned against the wall and watched as she lay in the bed watching tv, and before I knew it, I was out like a fucking light.

A loud ass snore scared me out of my sleep causing me to hit my head against the wall.

"Shit!" I snapped lowly.

My eyes shot to the crack in the door to see if I had woken anyone up. I was mad then a bitch when I saw Cassie all cuddled up with Sam's gay ass. I was even more mad at the fact that no one had caught me! Their sense of awareness is ass! I could've been a real intruder! I slowly crept out of the closet careful not to make any loud noises. Unable to resist, I slapped the fuck out of Sam and hauled ass out of the room.

His ass woke up whining like a little bitch, but I didn't stick around to see what happened next. I left the house and ran to my car. When I finally looked at my watch, I saw that it was damn near 4 in the morning. I shook my head and took my dumb ass home. At least I got a nut out of the shit.

Chapter Four

Cassie

Blow dryers, ratchet music and conversation filled the air as I walked around the shop, ensuring everything was perfect. I took the day off to get pampered with my girls, Genesis and Pilar. Rayne and Phoenix couldn't come today. Rayne is pregnant and the baby is kicking her ass. Phoenix was busy being under Xander's balls.

It wasn't often I had the chance to just sit and relax but today was a much-needed break. Between working to get my shop, raising Carlie alone, Sam and his annoying ass mama, and Jabari's looney ass, I AM BEAT! I just wanna sit here and unwind.

The shop's owner, *Denise*, had insisted I take the day off when I mentioned my sisters were coming in. Well, "sisters" might be a stretch, but over the past few months, reconnecting with Genesis and getting to know Pilar had made me feel like I'd gained a little family again.

"Cassie, you're supposed to be relaxing," Denise called from the front desk, giving me a playful glare.

Her short, curly hair bounced as she moved, and her bright red lipstick stood out against her dark brown skin.

"I can't help it." I called back with a grin, finally making my way to the pedicure area where Genesis and Pilar were already sipping mimosas waiting to get serviced.

"Look who finally decided to show up," Pilar teased, flipping her long, dark hair over her shoulder.

She was lounging in a plush chair, her legs crossed, and looking every bit like the queen she thought she was.

"Girl, I've been working!" I said, plopping down on the chair next to Genesis, who gave me a warm smile.

"You work too much. You're going to burn yourself out before you even get to open your spa." Genesis said softly with her eyes studying me.

I sighed, leaning back.

"I know, I know. But I have to save up. Carlie and I can't live on dreams, you know." I tried explaining.

Pilar rolled her eyes.

"You're too responsible, Cass. You need to let loose a little. That's why we're here. To make sure you relax and have a stress-free day." Pilar replied sassily.

A stylist appeared to start on Pilar's nails, and another began setting up Genesis' pedicure. I waved them off when they looked at me.

"I'll get mine done in a bit." I let them know since I was in no rush.

My mom had Carlie for the night so I was hoping I could get some one-on-one time with Sam later if you know what I mean.

Genesis sipped her drink, and her gaze landed on me.

"So, how's everything been since…you know?" She asked with a sneaky grin on her face.

The "you know" hung heavily in the air. She didn't need to say it. I knew exactly what her messy ass was referring to. Jabari showing up at my house unannounced has been the hot topic of our text thread ever since.

I groaned, covering my face with my hands.

"Pilarrrr why didn't you ever tell me how crazy your brother is?" I whined.

Pilar burst out laughing so hard she almost spilled her drink.

"Oh, this I have to hear. What did my sweet Jabari do now?" She asked through laughter.

Genesis looked a little sheepish, biting her lip.

"Listen! Sweet my ass! When Cassie called me and told me that man was there, I died! Pilar! Your brother broke into this girl's house and was chilling like he owned the place! I didn't even know he knew where she lived." Genesis exclaimed.

"Well, he does! And he made it very clear that I'd never be able to get away from him if I tried." I said, annoyed.

Pilar laughed even harder, clutching her stomach.

"That sounds like Jabari. Always so dramatic. He's never been interested in someone before so I'm excited to sit back and watch this shit unfold." Pilar replied excitedly.

"It's not funny. He scared the hell out of me." I muttered, though a small smile tugged at my lips despite myself.

"And then he had the nerve to lose his mind when he found out about Sam." I added.

That got Pilar's attention. She raised an eyebrow, smirking.

"Who is Sam and why am I just now hearing about him?" She asked.

I sighed, fiddling with the edge of my shirt.

"He's my uh... he's, my boyfriend. He's...he's a good guy." I revealed, almost letting my secret out.

"Good guy? Girl, a good guy wouldn't know what to do with yo ass." Pilar echoed, clearly unimpressed.

Before I could respond, the front door jingled, and a hush fell over the shop. I turned to see what had caused the sudden silence and felt my heart drop.

Jabari, Kenzo, and Adonis strolled in like they owned the place, commanding the attention of every woman. Literally every woman in the shop stopped what she was doing to stare, and I couldn't really blame them. Them niggas were...well, let's just say their looks weren't exactly subtle.

"What's good Cassie?" Kenzo said.

"What is do Sis?" Adonis also said.

"Hey Kenzo. Hey Adonis. I should've known y'all wouldn't let them out of your sights for long." I replied while playfully rolling my eyes.

Kenzo and Adonis both smirked before damn near attacking their wives making us all look on in admiration. Meanwhile, Jabari stood off to the side smirking at me. I did everything in my power to not show that I was affected, but baby the way my body acts when he is around should be investigated.

"Girl who is THAT?" one of the stylists whispered to Pilar, clearly smitten.

"None of your business. Jabari, what are you doing here?" I said quickly, standing up before Pilar could answer.

He smirked with his dark eyes locked on mine.

"Man, this is a spa, right? A nigga back is fucked up. Can you help me with that? And besides... I can't check on my favorite girl?" He asked.

I frowned because he seemed fine yesterday.

"What's wrong with your back?" I asked concerned.

"Yeah Bro. What's wrong with your back?" Kenzo asked with a smirk as if he knew something, making Jabari smack his lips.

"Aye, fuck you, messy ass nigga. Anyways, What's up Cassie? Can you help a nigga or naw?" He repeated.

The fuck was that about.

Genesis rolled her eyes.

"Jabari, leave her alone. She's had enough of your nonsense."

But he ignored her and began scanning my body as if he had x-ray vision. Just as I was beginning to get worked up, his gaze dropped to my hand making me panic internally.

"Where's yo little ring?" He asked cynically.

My stomach flipped as every head in the shop turned to me.

"Jabari, mind yo business." I said, my voice tight.

"You are my business. Now stop changing the subject Mama. Where is your engagement ring? You know, the one Sam gave you. You know, the cornball ass nigga you're supposed to be marrying?" He said casually, like he wasn't stirring up a storm.

The shop erupted in gasps and murmurs. Kenzo shook his head. Adonis laughed lowly and Pilar looked like she was going to burst out laughing again, and Genesis... Fuck!

Genesis looked hurt, even though she tried to play it off by busying herself with her drink. I knew her well enough to know that she was fucked up that I hadn't told her.

"You're engaged?" one of the stylists asked, wide-eyed.

I sighed, feeling myself getting annoyed by everyone's stares and questions.

"Yes, I'm engaged." I admitted.

"Since when?" Genesis asked quietly.

Her voice was barely audible over the chatter.

"It hasn't been long at all. I swear. I planned on telling you as soon as I wrapped my head around it." I pleaded.

My heart sank when I saw the flicker of pain in her eyes. The last thing I wanted to do was hurt my friend. I was honestly just trying to make sure this was a real thing before I told anyone. Hell, Jabari wouldn't even know if he wasn't breaking into people's houses and shit!

Pilar, of course, found the whole thing hilarious.

"This is fucking epic! Jabari finally finds someone who gives him a run for his money, and she's engaged to someone else. I love it." she said, wiping tears of laughter from her eyes.

Jabari, however, wasn't laughing. He stepped closer, his smirk fading into something more serious.

"Why didn't you tell anyone, Cassie? Embarrassed?" He asked accusingly.

My jaw tightened.

"No, I just…haven't gotten around to it. Not that it's any of your fucking business!" I snapped.

He chuckled, low and mocking.

"Riiiiiight. Sure." He replied.

The tension between us was so thick it was like trying to gargle peanut butter. As much as I wanted to turn up on his petty ass, I help myself back. I could feel Genesis and Pilar watching us closely and didn't want to make an even bigger scene in my workplace. I needed to get out of there before I said something I'd regret.

"Jabari, can we talk outside?" I said quietly.

I was so frustrated that my voice trembled with each word.

He raised an eyebrow but followed me out to the sidewalk. The cool air hit my face, but it didn't do shit to calm me down. I was HOT. I watched as he leaned against a blue Mercedes Benz that I assumed was his. With his huge arms folded and an impatient look on his face, he nodded at me as if telling me to speak.

"You had no right to air my business out like that." I snapped, turning to face him.

He shrugged, unbothered.

"What's the big deal? It's not like it's a secret. You said yes. Fuck are you hiding the shit for?" He asked.

The frown on his face only made him sexier with his ugly ass.

"I wasn't hiding shit. It was business to tell when I felt the need to. I know I said yes! Despite what you think in that small ass brain of yours, Sam makes me happy! Sam is…" I hissed.

"Not enough for you." He finished the sentence for me.

I froze, staring at him.

"That's not true." I said weakly, but even I didn't believe it.

He stepped closer and my heartbeat sped up.

"You're lying to yourself, Mama. And you know it." He said confidently.

My breath hitched as his gaze dropped to my lips, and for a moment, I forgot how to breathe. Just that quick, I forgot I was engaged and was ready to risk it all. His lips were so full and if I remember correctly soft as hell. The tension between us crackled like a live wire, and I hated how much I wanted him to close the distance between us.

But then he pulled back with his smirk returning.

"Don't worry, I won't tell them our *real* business Mama. I'll let you do that when you come to your senses." He joked.

And with that, he turned and walked away, leaving me standing there with my heart pounding in my chest and my coochie beat boxing in my pants.

Back inside, I said goodbye to everyone and then told Denise that I would come back for my services. She didn't ask questions. Instead, she just gave me a knowing look and a pat on the shoulder. I hopped in my car and immediately drove to the liquor store. I just wanted to go home and nurse a bottle of Sangria.

After quickly grabbing a few bottles of wine, I headed home. On the way, I decided to call my mom and Carlie. I knew my baby would cheer me up.

"Hey Mommy!" Carlie squealed as soon as the FaceTime connected.

She looked so much like me it was scary at times. She was so cute and innocent. Just that fast, my mood was lifted.

"Hey my Stinker! You having fun with your GG?" I asked happily.

"Yes! We made cookies and she let me do her makeup!" She replied excitedly making me laugh.

She always asked to my makeup and I shut that shit down every time. My mom was a sucka and gave in to everything.

"Sounds like fun Baby." I replied.

We chatted for a little while before my mom got on the phone. Her mother's radar must've gone off because she noticed immediately that something was off.

"You okay, sweetheart?" she asked, her eyes filled with concern.

"I'm fine, Mommy." I said quickly, avoiding her gaze.

Her lips pressed into a thin line, but she didn't push.

"You know I'm here if you want to talk." She offered.

"I know, Mommy. Thanks. Good night Carlie. I love y'all!" I sang.

"I love you too!" They replied before the call disconnected.

A few minutes later, I was pulling onto my street. My phone buzzed just as I pulled into the driveway. I groaned loudly when I saw that it was Sam.

"Hey." I said when I reluctantly answered.

"I was thinking I'd come over tonight. We haven't really talked since…you know." He replied.

I sighed, rubbing my temple. I really did not want to deal with this, but I went against my wishes and agreed.

"Sure, Sam. That's fine." I replied.

After I hung up, I sat in the car for a moment, staring at the house. My life felt like it was spinning out of control, and I didn't know how to stop it. I couldn't shake the feeling that everything was about to change—and not necessarily for the better.

CHAPTER Five

Jabari

Laughter rang out from the backyard as I walked up the stone path to Adonis and Pilar's house. I could already hear the chaos of my nephews before I even stepped through the gate.

"Bawi! Bawi" They cheered as soon as they saw me.

Two little bodies collided with my legs as soon as I appeared. Ameer and Xavier were identical terrors with a knack for causing mayhem wherever they went. They had inherited their mother's good looks and their father's troublemaking charm—a dangerous combination for two almost two-year-olds.

"What up my little niggas!" I grinned, scooping them both up at the same time, one in each arm.

Ameer immediately grabbed at my beard while Xavier pointed at the basketball I'd brought with me.

"Y'all been good today?" I asked, even though I already knew the answer.

"No!" they yelled in unison, giggling uncontrollably.

Pilar appeared in the doorway, her hands on her hips.

"Jabari, why do you hype them up every time you come over? I just got them to settle down." She fussed.

I smirked, setting the boys back on the ground.

"What can I say? I'm the fun uncle." I replied jokingly.

"Fun my ass." Pilar muttered, but there was no real heat behind her words.

Adonis came out behind her, holding a juice box in one hand and a wipe in the other. He looked like a man who hadn't had a peaceful moment in two years, but the pride in his eyes whenever he looked at his boys was undeniable.

"Jabari. What it do baby bro?" he greeted before handing off the juice box to Ameer, who immediately threw it to the ground making Adonis sigh.

"Ain't shit. Just came to chop it up with y'all." I said, shrugging as I followed them inside.

The house was in its usual state of organized chaos. Toys were scattered across the floor, and the twins had already resumed their mission of turning the living room into their personal jungle gym. Pilar handed me a drink as I sat on the couch, her eyes narrowing slightly.

"You're too quiet. What's going on?" she said, sitting across from me.

"Nothing." I simply said.

"Uh-huh." Pilar exchanged a glance with Adonis, who smirked as he sat down beside her.

"So... Cassie, huh?" Pilar asked, making me laugh.

"Mannnn you on some bullshit. What about her?" I asked.

"Don't play dumb. Don't forget I was at the shop the

other day. I saw that little performance you put on." Pilar said accusingly.

"You think THAT was a performance. That wasn't shit." I muttered, leaning back against the couch.

"Oh, it was a performance alright. You walked in that bitch like you were auditioning for a soap opera." Adonis said.

Pilar burst out laughing, leaning into her husband.

"I knew something was up when you mentioned her not having on her engagement ring. That girl's more rattled by you than she wants to admit." Pilar added.

"Not my problem," I said, keeping my tone neutral.

Pilar tilted her head, studying me.

"So, you're really about to sit yo slow ass in my face and act like you don't like her?" She asked.

I froze, glaring at her.

"I don't like shit. Look man, I didn't come here for the third degree. I came to chill with y'all and my nephews. Chill on the questions." I spat.

I hated being put in the hot seat. Especially when mufuckas knew I was lying.

"Uh-huh. You think I don't know you by now, Jabari? You've got it bad." she said again, grinning like the Cheshire cat.

Adonis chuckled, shaking his head.

"Man, I never thought I'd see the day. Jabari Creed caught up over a woman."

"I'm not caught up on shit." I snapped, but my voice lacked conviction.

"Sure, you're not. So, you're not going to care that Cassie and her fiancé are coming to the club tonight?" Pilar said, sipping her drink with a smug expression.

I sat up straighter, narrowing my eyes at her.

"Fuck are you talking about P?" I asked.

"Oh, didn't I mention it? Cassie finally decided to introduce Sam to everyone. I invited them to the club tonight." Pilar said innocently, batting her lashes.

Adonis barked out a laugh.

"You're messy as fuck Bae."

"Someone has to be." Pilar said with a shrug.

I clenched my jaw mad as fuck. The thought of Cassie bringing that clown around made my blood boil.

"Why would you do some shit like that?" I snapped.

"Why not? I didn't think you would care. You act like it's a big deal." Pilar replied sheepishly.

"It's not." I said quickly. Too quickly.

Adonis snorted.

"You're full of shit baby bro."

"Man, what time are y'all going?" I said, ignoring his comment.

"We're meeting at *EMOTIONS* at ten." Pilar said, clearly pleased with herself.

"Aight. I'll holla at y'all later." I said, standing abruptly.

Pilar smirked, leaning back in her seat.

"Don't do anything I wouldn't do, baby brother."

I rolled my eyes, grabbing my keys.

"Aye man fuck you yo! Besides there's not much you wouldn't do, Pilar." I shouted.

Adonis laughed as I headed for the door, his voice trailing after me.

"Try not to scare off the poor guy, Jabari."

I didn't respond, slamming the door behind me as I left.

Back at my place, I couldn't shake the irritation bubbling under my skin. The thought of Cassie bringing Sam around, acting like he belonged in her life, made my stomach churn more than I wanted to admit.

FLASHBACK: THE WEEKEND AFTER THE WEDDING

The suite was quiet, secluded, and damn near perfect. I leaned against the balcony railing, watching the sun dip low over the horizon. It was peaceful as fuck out here. However, that shit did nothing to ease my thoughts. My mind had a way of wandering in the silence, bringing up things I'd rather bury.

Behind me, I heard the soft padding of bare feet on the wooden floor. I turned just in time to see Cassie stepping out onto the balcony, wrapped in one of my shirts. I had just finished knocking the lining out of her pussy and thought she would be sleep for the night. The sight of her in my clothes made me want to go for another round or two. Shit!

"You okay?" she asked, breaking me out of my trance.

I nodded as my gaze lingered on her.

"Yeah, just thinking." I replied.

She came closer, leaning her hip against the railing beside me. The way the wind played with her hair, the way her skin seemed to glow in the fading sunlight—it was enough to make a nigga forget his own name.

"You're quiet. That's not normal." she said, tilting her head to look at me.

I smirked, shaking my head.

"And here I thought women liked the strong, silent type." I joked.

Cassie rolled her eyes, but her smile betrayed her amusement.

"Maybe but stop reflecting. What's on your mind?" She asked.

I hesitated. I wasn't used to opening up to anyone outside of my family. She was trying to pull something out of me that I wasn't used to sharing.

"My father..." I said finally.

Cassie's smile faded, replaced by a look of concern.

"What about him?"

I let out a slow breath, my eyes now fixed on the horizon.

"He died when I was nine. Fuck ass police killed him right in front of us." I revealed.

Her gasp was soft, almost inaudible, but I heard it. I felt it.

"They said it was an accident. Said he was reaching for a weapon. But they fucking lied. I was there. I saw the whole thing." I continued.

I clenched my jaw, the memory so sharp that it felt like it was happening all over again.

"He literally answered the door, and they had their guns drawn, yelling at him to get on the ground. He didn't even get the chance to respond before they shot him." I explained.

Cassie reached out and brushed her fingers against my arm. It was a small gesture, but it anchored me, keeping me from spiraling too far into the past.

"I'm so sorry, Jabari," she said full of sorrow.

I nodded, swallowing hard.

"I tried to hold it together after that, but it wasn't easy. Losing him changed everything for me and Pilar. I think that's why I am the way I am now. I don't trust people. Don't let them get close. It's easier that way." I explained.

Cassie was quiet for a moment, her eyes searching mine.

"You're not as closed off as you think," she said softly.

I raised an eyebrow, smirking despite myself.

"Oh yeah? And what makes you think that?" *I quizzed.*

"Because you're telling me this," *she said simply.*

I couldn't argue with that.

"What about you? What skeletons are you hiding?" *I asked, wanting to shift the focus off me.*

Cassie hesitated, and for a moment, I thought she wasn't going to answer. But then she sighed, her gaze dropping to the ground.

"I was in a relationship with Carlie's father for three years..." *she began saying before pausing to collect herself.*

"His name was Danny. At first, he was everything I thought I wanted—charming, funny, attentive. But as soon as he was sure he had me, he changed."

Her voice wavered, and I felt a surge of anger toward a man I'd never met.

"He became controlling, angry, violent." *she continued.*

"He'd yell at me, call me names, hit me if I talked back. Hell, he hit me whenever he felt like it. No matter what he did though, I stayed. I stayed because I didn't think I deserved better."

Her shoulders shook, and I realized she was crying. Without thinking, I pulled her into my arms, holding her tightly.

"One night, he accused me of something so stupid and almost killed me. He choked me until I passed out and fucking raped me while I was unconscious." *she said, her voice muffled against my chest.*

That nigga was a dead man walking! On my momma and my daddy!

"When I woke up, I was in the hospital and that's when I found out I was pregnant. That was the last straw. Luckily for me, he didn't get the chance to fight me on it because he was *killed while I was still in the hospital recovering."* She finished saying while still sobbing.

I cupped her face, forcing her to look at me.

"Cassie, listen to me. That man was a coward and a piece of shit. He is lucky somebody got to him before I did. None of what he did was your fault, and you deserve so much better." I spat.

Her eyes searched mine, filled with doubt and something else —something fragile.

"Sometimes I don't feel like I do." she admitted.

"Then let me remind you." I said, my voice low.

I kissed her, slow and deliberately, pouring everything I couldn't put into words into that single moment. She melted against me, her hands clutching at my shirt as if I were the only thing keeping her grounded.

The next morning, sunlight streamed through the curtains, casting a glow across the room. Cassie was still asleep, curled up beside me with her head resting on my chest.

I ran my fingers through her hair, admiring how peaceful she looked. It was the complete opposite of the vulnerability she'd shown the night before. The tears and confessions that had made me see her in a completely different light.

I thought about the way she'd opened up to me, about the strength it must have taken for her to want to leave Danny and start over on her own. It made me respect her even more than I already did, and that was saying something.

My phone buzzed on the nightstand, breaking the moment. I reached for it, careful not to wake her, and saw a text from Pilar.

Big Sis: *Where are you? You are missing all the festivities nigga!*

I smirked, shaking my head. She was relentless.

Cassie stirred beside me, her eyes fluttering open.

"What time is it?" She asked.

"Early. Go back to sleep." I said, setting my phone back down.

She smiled sleepily, nuzzling closer to me.

"You're so warm." She moaned.

I chuckled before wrapping my arm around her tighter.

"And you're clingy." I added.

"Shut up." she mumbled, making me laugh.

As she drifted back to sleep, I couldn't help but wonder what the hell I was going to do about her.

Because the truth was, I wasn't ready to let her go.

―――

Snapping out of my flashback, I opened my closet, pulling out a black AMIRI shirt and a pair of dark jeans. If she was going to show up with her fiancé, I was going to remind her exactly who the fuck I was.

By the time I was dressed and ready, the anger had simmered into something colder, more calculated. Tonight wasn't just about seeing Cassie. Nah. It was about making sure she knew that Sam didn't belong in the same world as her.

And if I had to play dirty to make that point, so fucking be it.

CHAPTER Six

CASSIE

I ADJUSTED the strap of my black satin dress for the third time, frowning at my reflection in the full-length mirror. The dress clung to my curves, stopping just above my knees, and the neckline dipped just enough to make me feel sexy but not overly exposed. I paired it with gold heels and matching accessories, but no matter how much I adjusted myself, I couldn't shake the nerves twisting in my stomach.

"Mommy, you look like a princess!" Carlie's voice piped up from behind me.

I turned to see her standing in the doorway of my bedroom, her wide amber eyes full of admiration.

"Thank you, baby," I said, scooping her up and twirling her around.

Her giggles were the only thing keeping my anxiety at bay.

As I set her down, I noticed her tiny backpack packed and sitting near the door.

"You ready to go fun with Mr. and Mrs. Drakos?"

Carlie nodded eagerly.

"Xavier and Ameer are gonna be there too, right? And Zahra? And Lorenzo? Ooh! And Kenzi and KJ?" She asked excitedly, making me giggle.

"Yes, ma'am. You're gonna have so much fun." I replied with a smile.

"Who's Zahra?" Sam interrupted.

I glanced up to see him standing in the doorway, adjusting the cufflinks on his shirt. He looked handsome in a crisp white button-up and tailored black slacks, but his tone carried that familiar edge that always made me tense.

"She's one of the kids. Adara and Sayid are watching all of them tonight so we can go out." I replied, forcing my tone to remain even.

Sam frowned.

"I don't know why you're so eager to leave her with people you barely know." He bitched.

"They're not strangers, Sam. Genesis introduced me to them months ago. They're family to her, and they offered to help." I said, already tired of this argument.

"Still..." he muttered, straightening his tie.

I sighed, turning back to Carlie.

"Go grab your shoes, sweetie. Mr. Drakos will be here soon." I instructed.

She darted off, leaving me alone with Sam, who was now scrutinizing me with narrowed eyes.

"Is that what you're wearing?" he asked.

His tone dripped with disapproval. You would've thought I was wearing a thong and a smile the way he was mugging me.

I blinked at him, confused as fuck.

"Yes, it is. What's wrong with my outfit?" I asked annoyedly.

"It's a bit much, don't you think?" He replied.

"It's a fucking club, Sam. What did you expect me to wear? A church dress? A warm-up suit?" I said, crossing my arms.

He scowled but didn't respond, and I took the moment to grab my clutch and double-check that I had everything.

A knock at the door saved me from whatever comment he was about to make, and I hurried to answer it.

Sayid stood on the other side, looking intimidating and handsome as ever. He gave me a polite nod before his dark eyes shifted to Sam, who was lingering in the background.

"Mr. Drakos. Nice to see you as always." I greeted him before stepping aside to let him in.

"Hey Cassie," he said simply.

His voice was so deep that I damn near jumped when he spoke. Before anyone could say another word, Carlie came running into the room with her shoes in hand.

"Hi, Papa Drakos!" she chirped, throwing her arms around his leg.

"Hey, little one." he said, the faintest hint of a smile softening his features.

I was shocked to hear her call him "Papa Drakos". Obviously, I was on the late show because Sayid didn't mind or try to correct her. This must not be a new thing.

"Papa?" Sam tried mumbling, but unfortunately for him, we all heard him.

"Yeah, you got a problem with that nigga?" Sayid barked.

I almost pissed myself when he said that shit and he wasn't even talking to me. Knowing that Sam wouldn't stand a chance against the old man, I quickly stepped in.

"He... he was just joking. Uh, her bag is all packed. Thank you again for watching her." I stuttered, handing it to him.

He nodded, but his eyes never left Sam, looked like he was about to shit his pants. Then, without another word to me or Sam, he turned and scooped Carlie up in one arm. "Let's go, princess."

"Bye, Mommy!" Carlie waved as they left.

Her excitement warmed my heart despite the tension in the air.

As soon as the door closed, I felt Sam's presence behind me.

"Did you see the way he looked at me? Or hear what he said to me?" he asked angrily.

I turned to face him, already tired of this conversation before it even started.

"He didn't say anything wrong, Sam. You were out of line." I spat.

"Out of line! Are you fucking kidding me?" he shouted.

I found it hilarious how he all of a sudden had a voice now but was quiet as a church mouse when Sayid was here.

I shook my head, grabbing my clutch and heading toward the door.

"If it meant so much to you then you should've said something when he was here. Don't expect me to speak up for you when you couldn't do the shit yourself. Look, let's just go. We're already late." I barked before walking out on his ass.

If he came, he came. If not, oh fucking well at this point!

By the time we arrived at the club, my nerves were on fire. The bass from the music vibrated through my body as we entered, and I scanned the room, spotting Genesis, Pilar, and the others near a VIP section. It felt good that everyone came just to meet my fiancé. Granted, I was hoping no one showed up. Nonetheless, it made me happy that they cared.

As we approached, I saw Jabari first, and of course, he was surrounded by women. He sat back in the booth like he owned the place, his arm draped lazily over the backrest, and a drink in his hand. The women around him were all leaning in, vying for his attention, but his eyes met mine the second we walked in.

My breath caught in my throat and my heart dropped to my pinky toe. He looked the fuck good. Too fucking good. A black button-up, the top two buttons undone, sleeves rolled up to his elbows. The dim lighting made his caramel skin glow, and his dark eyes were focused on me only. I needed to have a talk with my pussy because she needs to know who her fiancé is!

"Cassie!" Pilar called out, waving us over.

I forced myself to smile, ignoring the way my heart was pounding, and led Sam toward the group.

Introductions were made, and Sam was polite enough.

"It's so good to finally meet you Sam. What do you do for work? Do you have any kids? Tell us about yourself." Genesis asked eagerly.

"Damn Bae! Let the nigga ask one question before you ask another one. You acting like the feds in this bitch." Kenzo joked making everyone laugh.

"It's okay. I'm a marketing specialist and no, I don't have any kids. Nor do I plan on having any." Sam replied while laughing.

I, on the other hand, frowned because that was news to me. We never discussed kids, but he's also never told me that he didn't want any. That's definitely something we will need to talk about later because I don't fuck with that at all. Being an only child was not fun at all, and I plan on having at least three more kids in the near future.

Genesis could see that his answer bothered me, so she changed the subject. I love that she knows me without me having to say anything.

"That's what's up. Well, let's take some shots and enjoy this kid free night. I know I am! I love my babies but them little fuckers are terrible!" She said dramatically.

Laughter spilled over the table as Kenzo and Genesis fussed about their kids and their behavior. Kenzo refused to believe that his kids were bad, but we all knew the truth. They were adorable little demons! Hell, Pilar and Adonis' twins were worse, and they knew it! That's why they didn't bother chiming in.

The night was going good as everyone drank, sang, and danced. Everyone except Sam that it. I could feel his hand tightening on mine every time Jabari so much as glanced in our direction. All he had to do was relax. He was making the shit awkward, and I was feeling suffocated.

At one point, Sam leaned in close, his lips brushing against my ear.

"Who is he and why the fuck does he keep staring at you?" he asked, his tone accusatory.

I stiffened, pulling back slightly.

"Who are you talking about?" I feigned ignorance.

I knew damn well who he was talking about!

"You know who! Don't insult my intelligence, Cassie." he hissed.

Before I could respond, Jabari appeared out of nowhere. I could tell by the smirk on his face that he was about to piss me off.

"Everything okay over here?" He asked.

Sam straightened, and his grip on my arm tightened.

"We're fine." Sam answered.

Jabari's gaze dropped to Sam's hand on my arm, and his smirk widened.

"You sure about that?" He asked tauntingly.

"Jabari." I said warningly, trying to diffuse the situation.

"What? I was just checking on you, Mama." He said innocently, taking a sip of his drink.

Sam's eyes narrowed.

"Mama? The fuck? Is there something I should know?" He barked.

I felt a flush of heat crawl up my neck as Jabari raised an eyebrow at me, clearly amused. If I knew I would win, I would steal off on his punk ass.

"You need to chill, Sam. Jabari is just joking around." I snapped.

Sam wasn't convinced, and his mood only worsened when one of the women from the booth sauntered over, pressing herself against Jabari and giggling.

"You're popular tonight, Daddy." she purred, running a manicured finger down his chest.

Jabari didn't even glance at her. His eyes were locked on me.

"Yeah, but there is only care about one person in this room who has my attention." he said smoothly.

My stomach flipped, and I hated how easily he got under my skin.

Sam's hand slid to my waist, pulling me closer.

"Let's go get a drink." He said sharply.

"Yeah. Good idea." I said quickly, needing to get away from Jabari and his petty comments.

As we walked away, I could still feel his eyes on me, and it made my legs shake. Fucking Jabari.

Sam's bitchy attitude didn't improve as the night went on. He was watching me like a hawk. His hand never left my waist or arm. I guess he thought I might run off at any moment or some shit. Like we didn't fucking come here together.

"Why are you acting like this? I thought we were having a good time." I finally asked.

He was so bothered by Jabari that he wanted to stay seated at the bar instead of going back to the VIP section. I wanted to leave his mad ass there, but I stayed with him so he wouldn't have a bitch fit.

"Why are *you* acting like this?" he shot back.

"Like the fuck what?" I spat.

"Like you're trying to get his attention. No wonder you decided to dress like that!" he said, his eyes narrowing.

My mouth dropped open in shock.

"Excuse me?"

"You heard me. You're dressed like you're trying to impress someone, and it sure as hell isn't me." he said, his jaw tight.

I began to hyperventilate a bit as I recalled the times Danny would act this same way. It never ended pretty. My fear only lasted for a moment when I realized I was no longer that scared little girl. Also, because I knew no one would allow Sam to harm me. He would get his ass beat the fuck up. That alone gave me the battery pack I needed to let his ass have it.

"First of fucking all, I wore this for *me*, Sam. Not for you, not for Jabari, and certainly not for anyone else in this damn club." I shouted over the music.

Out of the corner of my eye, I saw movement, and my heart sank as Jabari approached yet again.

"Everything okay over here?" he asked me, but his eyes were on Sam.

"Why do you keep getting in our damn business. You act like you're her bodyguard or something." Sam snapped, glaring at him.

Jabari smirked before placing his hands in his pockets.

"Nigga I'll be her bodyguard, her man or whatever else she needs me to be in this bitch." Jabari replied tauntingly.

"I swear to God..." Sam started, but I cut him off.

"Would you both fucking stop it! I didn't come here for this shit!" I said firmly, stepping between them.

Jabari's smirk widened, but he didn't say anything else. I hated how Jabari could get under my skin. How he could make me question everything with just a few words. But most of all, I hated how much I wanted to sit on his fucking face... Again.

CHAPTER Seven

Jabari

The second I saw Sam grab her arm, I knew I was about to fuck some shit up. There I was minding mine and Cassie's business in VIP, surrounded by some hoes whose names I didn't give a fuck to learn. They were only here to make Cassie jealous and from the way she'd been mugging us, I would say they served their purpose.

I'd been keeping an eye on Cassie all night, pretending like I didn't notice her, but I noticed every fucking thing. The way her ass sat up in that dress, how it bounced like a basketball every time she took a step, the way she would bite her top lip and shift her weight to one leg when her bitch boy said something to annoy her, and even the nervous way she'd glance my way only to quickly look away when I caught her.

And then there was this nigga... Sam. Clinging to her like a damn shadow and scowling at anyone who dared to glance her way. It pissed me off that he was acting like she was his property. She didn't belong to him, and they both knew that shit. I don't even know why she's wasting both of their times, but I guess.

It was one thing to watch her from afar and play my little games, flirting with women I didn't even want just to see if I could get a reaction out of her. But it was another thing to see his hand gripping her arm, his face too close to hers. His lips were moving too fast and the scowl on his face let me know that he was pressing her. Some shit he should've never attempted around me.

Before I even realized what I was doing, I was on my feet.

"Jabari," Pilar's voice called after me, but I ignored her.

"Yeeeaaahhh! Go get yo woman! I fucking raised you nigga!" Zeke cheered, but I ignored his ass too.

As I approached, I saw the way Cassie's face twisted in anger and frustration, but it was the look of fear in her eyes that pushed me over the edge. Knowing her past and what she had already overcome, I'll be damned if I sit back and watch a mufucka put any type of fear in her heart.

Sam turned to face me, his hand still gripping her arm.

"Like Cassie said, we didn't come here for this shit. So, I'll ask you again to mind your damn business and run along." he said, his tone just as sharp.

"Oh, is that right? Because it looks like you're about two seconds away from making it my business," I said, my eyes narrowing.

Cassie began pleading with me through her eyes, but she didn't say anything.

"I see you're hard of hearing." Sam growled, stepping in front of her as if to shield her from me.

I had to give it to him. He had some balls. I stood about 4 inches taller and weighed at least 75 pounds more than him. Yet, he didn't back down. He's brave. Dumb as fuck, but brave, nonetheless.

"Aight y'all. Let's chill. We were having a good time. Cassie, come take a shot with me." Genesis walked up saying.

"No, Cassie is gonna grab her things so we can leave. We should've never come here in the first place!" Sam barked.

"Aye, Bitch if you want to keep your fucking chin attached to your face, I suggest you watch the way you speak to my wife." Kenzo shouted.

I bit back my laughter when I heard Zeke start cracking up.

"Thi... this is my fiancé. I was only telling her..." Sam tried saying, but Kenzo cut him off.

"You weren't telling her shit! If you want to leave, then go mufucka! Ain't nobody holding you hostage. But if Sis wants to stay then that's what the fuck she's going to do! Now fuck around and find out if you want to! I shoot niggas like you for fun." Kenzo threatened.

"Hey! It's okay Kenzo. Thank you! I'm going to head out. I have a damn headache all of a sudden." Cassie chimed in while rolling her eyes.

I was pissed that she was letting his weak ass win. I could tell she didn't want to go, but she was also embarrassed. I would be too if my fiancé acted an ass like he did.

"You know you don't have to leave with this nigga, right?" I asked her.

Sam laughed bitterly.

"Oh my God! Who the hell are you? The ex-boyfriend who can't let go? Or just another nigga trying to get some pussy?" He asked.

It seemed like the music stopped and all conversation had ended. Before I knew it, my fist was connecting with his jaw, sending him stumbling backward.

"Jabari!" Cassie screamed.

Sam recovered quickly, lunging toward me, but Zeke stepped in and pushed his ass back. My brothers knew I didn't need any assistance, so I knew Zeke only stood up to stop me from killing this nigga. These hands were trained to go. He's lucky I only swung one time.

"Say that shit again and watch I break your fucking face bitch ass nigga!" I said through gritted teeth, my chest heaving.

"Fuck you!" Sam shouted, his face red with anger.

"Aye, I knew tonight would be lit!" Xander shouted excitedly.

"Xander hush!" Phoenix snapped.

"Pilare, sit the hell down! That man don't need your help fighting!" Adonis shouted.

I hadn't even seen my sister get up, but I should've known she would be on go. She don't play about me and vice versa.

"I know he don't, but I'm gone stand here to be fucking sure!" Pilar snapped.

"Stop it! Everybody! Please!" Cassie's voice cut through the chaos, and she stepped between us.

She placed her hands against my chest to keep me back. I froze at her touch, but if she thought it would calm me down, she was highly mistaken. Sam had me heated and if he didn't leave soon, she was going to see a whole other side to me.

"Please. Just stop." she said, her voice trembling.

For a moment, it was just the two of us. Her eyes were pleading with me to let it go. And then she turned to Sam.

"Let's fucking go. Now!" she said, her voice steadier now.

Sam looked stunned, his mouth opening and closing like he couldn't believe what he was hearing.

"Cassie—"

"Don't. Let's... Go!" she said, cutting him off.

She turned back to me, and I couldn't decipher the look on her face. It bothered me that I was worried if she was mad at me or not. I didn't do shit wrong! If anything, I handled myself well. Any other time, I would've shot him in the neck.

Before she could walk away, I grabbed her arm to leave her with a nice message. I leaned down so that I could speak directly into her ear.

"Don't fuck that nigga Cassie." I said sternly.

"Excuse me?! That nigga is my fiancé! And besides, this is my pussy!" She snapped.

"I don't give a fuck about that cheap ass ring on your finger! If you give that nigga MY PUSSY, I'm chopping him into pieces and feeding him to my tiger!" I yelled.

She smacked her lips and rolled her eyes hard as if I gave a fuck.

"You don't even have a fucking tiger Jabari!"

"See! That's yo fucking problem! You always worried about the wrong shit!" I replied annoyedly.

"Boy, fuck you!" Was all she said before storming off with her bitch ass dude behind her.

I watched her walk away, her heels clicking against the floor. Her stance was steady, but I knew she was holding herself together by a thread. I could tell by how she was clutching her purse against her midsection. Plus, she didn't even tell anyone bye.

And then she was gone. On my mama she better not be mad at me or I'm beating the fuck out of Sam!

The rest of the night at the club was unbearable. These niggas didn't waste no time going in on my shit. I swear they were just as messy as their damn wives. My sister included! Had she not invited Cassie and dude ass, none of this shit would've happened.

It was Zeke who started his shit first.

"You lucky I stepped in when I did. Lucious Lyon was finna whoop yo ass!"

The entire table started cracking up including me. That nigga did look like Terrence Howard back in his "Best Man" days.

"Yeah, I thought you were about to take your first L baby bro." Adonis added.

"Man, y'all got me fucked up!" I replied while still laughing with them.

"Was that your bitch or something?" One of the chicks that I had been entertaining asked.

While another said, "Yeah, I could've sworn you said you were single! That sure looked like boyfriend behavior to me!"

I think her name is Kimber or some shit. Bitch face was a solid 5, but that ass sat up better than two bunk beds!

"I swear I hope you know how to fight." Genesis calmly said.

Aww shit.

"Excuse me?" Kimber (Maybe) asked with a little too much dip on her mufuckin chip.

"I asked if you knew how to fight because that bitch you were speaking on is my muthafuckin sister. She's not here to defend herself, but I am. So, watch your fucking mouth or I'll show you that you can't fight!" Genesis snapped.

The entire time she spoke, Kenzo stared at her like a proud parent.

"Girl..." Kimber tried replying but was cut off.

"Girl nothing. Bari get this bitch out of our section, before I show her the real meaning of standing on bitches' necks." Pilar threatened.

Zeke, Xander and Kenzo started cracking up while Adonis and I quickly jumped into action because we knew she was dead ass serious.

"Aye, you hoes gotta go!" Adonis shouted.

"Hoes!" The women yelled simultaneously while looking at me crazy as if I was supposed to save they asses.

"The fuck are y'all looking at him for!" Genesis yelled.

"Right! Bye mufucka!" Rayne added.

Her ass had been so quiet all night I forgot she was even here!

"I've been wanting to beat a bitch. I'm with all this dumb shit." Phoenix said, making me laugh.

She was so quiet normally so it was nice to know that she would be on bullshit like the rest of us.

"Aye man, y'all heard the man. Get the fuck out!" I yelled.

They talked shit the entire way, but them hoes got out of that section.

After they were gone, we all had a few more drinks before we decided to call it a night. I felt out of place like a mufucka. All these niggas were basically fucking their wives as if I wasn't sitting right the fuck there. Since everyone was parked next to each other, we all walked to the lot and waited until the women were safe in the whips, before they started clowning me A-FUCKIN-GAIN!

"Alright nigga. Get home safe and please know that I'm clowning yo bitch ass tomorrow." Kenzo said playfully.

"The fuck for?" I asked.

"Nigga you've been acting like a damn fool all night. You used to bitch every chance you got about us being in love and now look at yo ass! Fucking whipped!" Xander said, crossing his arms.

"You crazy as hell! I ain't ever been in love and never will! I just fuck with Cassie. That's all." I said sharply.

"That's all huh? Nigga you love the fuck out of that girl. You were ready to knock that dude's head off back there." Adonis scoffed.

"Because he deserved it." I said while shrugging.

"Did he though? I would've been mad too had you been staring at my woman all night and constantly getting in our shit!" Kenzo replied.

I didn't even know how to reply because I knew that I had forced it all night, but I honestly didn't give a fuck.

"Fuck all that shit, nigga what you gone do?" Zeke asked, leaning forward.

"I'm not gone do shit. She's engaged." I snapped, my voice rising.

"And nigga! What the fuck does that mean?" Kenzo asked, his tone skeptical.

"Man, I'll holla at y'all later." I said through gritted teeth, before hopping in my car and dipping.

On the way home, I decided to pull up Cassie's cameras and see if that nigga had gone home with her. When I saw her house was empty, I got pissed the fuck off. Where the fuck was she? I checked her location on her phone, and it showed that she was at that nigga's house.

"Okay, she thinks I'm playing! I got something for that ass." I said aloud while smirking.

I pulled up to Cassie's house on pure bullshit. Now, I could've went to Sam's house and raised hell, but I had something better for her little hardheaded ass. I bet after tonight she will see that I about what I be talking about!

I walked right into her house using the key that I had made and took my shoes off at the door. I went straight to her bedroom because I was on a mission. Any other time, I would see if she had something in the fridge to eat. Hell, she feeds me more than she knows. I stay coming in this mufucka.

Once I was in her bedroom, I made sure I was at a good angle for the camera that I had set up in her room. I needed this to be a motion picture film. After looking on my phone and seeing that I was indeed in a spot, I began my show.

I started taking all of my clothes off while staring directly at the camera.

"Damn Cassie. I wish you were here right now Mama.

Look how hard my dick is just thinking about yo sexy ass." I said lowly while stroking my dick.

Then I went and laid on the bed and got comfortable. I reached inside of her nightstand and grabbed her rose toy that she liked to use. I put the toy to my nose and took a big ass whiff.

"Mmmm! Shit smells just like you. Sweet as fuck." I groaned.

While smelling and licking her rose, I started beating my meat right on her bed. All I could picture was her fat juicy pussy suffocating my dick and it had me about to cum already. Her pussy tasted better than my favorite fruit. I would eat that mufucka all day and night. I stroked my dick faster and took another lick at her toy and that was all she wrote.

"Fuckkkk! Mama! That pussy tastes so fucking good! I need you to sit on my fucking face. Ride my face, Mama! Who needs fucking oxygen! Smother me shit!" I moaned.

I wasn't a quiet nigga in the bedroom. I was very vocal and Cassie loved that shit. I made sure to stare right into the camera too when I wasn't closing my eyes.

"Here it comes Mama. Come catch this nut!" I yelled before placing the rose by my dick and nutting all over that mufucka.

"Ooh shit! I needed that!" I moaned.

I laid there for a while spent. That nut took a lot out of me. As much as I wanted to take my ass to sleep, I knew I needed to get home. I reluctantly got up from her bed and went to clean myself up in her bathroom. After redressing, I left the house and took my ass home. Oh, I left the rose right on her bed too, still covered in my kids.

Once I was home, I took a quick shower and ran to my

room like an excited ass kid. I grabbed my phone from my dresser and went to the videos from Cassie's house. Once I found the clip I was looking for, I saved it to my phone. After cropping it to the parts I wanted shown, I sent the video to Cassie.

I knew she would trip the fuck out when she saw it, I didn't give a fuck. I also knew she would want this dick too. I hated to reveal my access to her house so soon, but I was desperate. She actually told that nigga she would marry him. That shit can't happen. Nah. That shit won't happen. I bet my life on that!

Chapter Eight

Cassie

I woke up this morning to a thick, suffocating silence. I could feel the heat radiating from the other side of the bed where Sam lay with his back to me, scrolling on his phone. I rolled over slowly, my body aching from exhaustion, both physical and emotional.

Last night was a fucking disaster! The confrontation at the club, the way he grabbed my arm, the argument that followed… all of it was replaying in my head like a broken record. And now, lying next to him, I couldn't shake the feeling that shit was only about to get worse.

I stared at the ceiling, counting the cracks in the paint and wondering how much longer I could keep up this charade of normalcy. The argument from last night that we had when we arrived at Sam's house echoed in my mind, sharp and bitter like the taste of cheap whiskey.

"You just stood there and let him humiliate me, Cassandra. Do you know how fucking embarrassing that was?" Sam had said, his voice cracking because of his bruised ego.

"I didn't let shit happen! You think I wanted Jabari to punch you?" I snapped back in disbelief.

It didn't matter what I said to this man. He was convinced I had sided with Jabari, or that I secretly enjoyed seeing him put Sam on his ass or something.

"You embarrassed me. You let that thug talk to me like that, and then you just walked away. Do you have any idea how that made me look?" He shouted.

"That thug is my friend. And maybe if you hadn't grabbed my arm like that, none of it would've happened." I yelled.

My patience was nonexistent at this point. I was the fuck over it.

His laugh was bitter, and full of disdain.

"Oh, so now it's my fault? You dressed like that, flaunting yourself in front of everyone, yet I'm the bad guy?" He asked.

I felt my jaw tighten, anger bubbling up inside me.

"I dressed like that because I wanted to feel good about myself, Sam. Not for you, not for anyone else. For me. It's never a problem any other time I dress like this!" I replied.

He had me so fucked up!

"Yeah, well, it didn't look like it was just for you." he muttered, before he started taking his clothes off.

I stared at him completely stunned. I couldn't believe that nigga!

"You know what, Sam? Maybe the problem isn't how I dress or who I'm friends with. Maybe the problem is your ass." I finally replied.

He spun around, his eyes narrowing.

"What's that supposed to mean?"

"It means you've been nothing but controlling and condescending lately, and I'm fucking tired of it." I spat furiously.

"Controlling? You're unbelievable." he barked out a laugh, shaking his head.

"And you're a dick who is about to be one less fiancé if he doesn't get his shit together!" I shouted before leaving the room.

I went to his living room and stayed there until I was sure his ass was sleeping. Only then did I go back into his room and took my ass to sleep.

―――

"Morning," I mumbled, my voice hoarse from sleep and the yelling I did the night before.

Sam didn't respond immediately. When he finally turned to face me, his expression was cold, his eyes hard.

"Morning," he said flatly.

I sighed, sitting up and pulling the sheets around me.

"Look, about last night—"

"Don't. I don't want to hear it." He cut me off rudely.

I blinked at him, startled by his abruptness. "Excuse me?"

"You will never admit your wrongdoings so what the hell are we talking about it for?" He bitched.

I sighed in exhaustion and swung my legs over the side of the bed. I shivered as my feet brushed against the cold hardwood floor. I glanced at Sam one last time, noting the way his shoulders were hunched in annoyance and resentment and knew to just drop the whole fucking thing.

I need some space.

"I'm going to the bathroom," she said softly, more to the room than to him.

No response.

I smacked my lips in irritation and stomped to his

bathroom grabbing my phone from his nightstand on the way. I swear the bathroom felt like a sanctuary. I locked the door, leaning against it as I let out a shaky breath. As much as I wanted to go the fuck off, I knew nothing good would come of it.

Sitting on the toilet, I pulled out my phone, hoping for a distraction. As I scrolled through my notifications, I noticed I had missed calls and plenty text messages from Genesis and the other girls. However, a text from an unknown number was what caught my attention.

My brows furrowed as I opened it. At first, I didn't understand what I was looking at. It looked to be a video, but what was alarming was the location looked like my damn room. The video began to play, and my breath hitched as realization dawned.

It was fucking Jabari.

He was in my house... In *my bedroom*. The video showed him lying on my bed, his naked ass body sprawled lazily across my side. I just washed those fucking sheets!

Throwing caution to the wind, I quickly turned the water on at the sink to drown out the sounds. I needed to see this video. I needed to hear him too. After putting my volume on low, I turned my phone to the side to expand the screen.

"That pussy tastes so fucking good! I need you to sit on my fucking face." He moaned.

My pussy instantly started contracting and I knew then that I was just as crazy as he was. This man not only broke into my house but is masturbating on my bed and my hot ass is ready to fuck.

Watching him smell and lick my rose had me jealous. I never wanted to be a toy so bad in my life!

I stared intensely as he stroked his dick nice and slowly. His dick was huge! And it was so fucking pretty. I still have a slight ache in the back of my throat from letting him fuck my face the night of the wedding. The entire time he stroked his dick on my bed I envisioned him fucking my face again.

"Fuck!" I whispered harshly.

I hadn't even noticed that my free hand was no longer free. I unintentionally reached into my panties and began rubbing my clit vigorously. His voice was so low and husky as he murmured my name. It sent shivers down my spine.

"Here it comes Mama. Come catch this nut!" He moaned loudly and I watched as he nutted all over my damn rose.

I swear it was like I was possessed! That was all it took for me to cum all over my hand.

"Ahhhh! Shiiiit! Bari Fuck!" I cried out quietly.

I sat there and attempted to calm myself down. That nut had taken a lot out of me. The longer I sat there collecting myself, the angrier I became.

How does he keep getting into my damn house? How did he know I wasn't there? How long has he been doing this shit? Although I enjoyed the climax, my mind was now racing, and I was pissed the fuck off.

But... beneath my anger was something I fucking hated even more: the fact that I wished I was there at that same moment with him.

The video ended with Jabari smirking into the camera.

His eyes bore into the lens as if he were staring right at me. Beneath the video, was a message that read:

Unknown: *I'm ready when you are Mama*

My hands trembled as I locked my phone. My breath came in short bursts, and I couldn't get a grip on which emotion I felt most. I felt violated, enraged, confused, and —God help me—horny, jealous, miserable, and nostalgic.

"I need to get home," I whispered to myself with my voice shaking.

After wiping myself, and washing my hands, I returned to the bedroom with a face that I hoped was carefully blank.

"Take me home," I demanded, slipping on my shoes.

Sam looked up from his phone, his brows furrowing.

"What now? You're just going to leave without talking about last night?" he asked, irritation clear in his voice.

"Boy fuck you! I tried to talk, and you didn't want to. So now, I don't want to. Are you going to take me or not? I need to get home." I repeated firmly.

"To do what? Avoid this conversation? Or is it because of him?" He barked accusingly.

That was it! He had officially pushed me over the edge.

"I'm starting to think you want that nigga! You bring him up more than me! I'm not thinking about that fucking man (LIE)! Get that shit through your fucking head! This isn't about Jabari! It's about my daughter. Carlie's being dropped off soon, and I need to be there!" I shouted.

Sam scoffed, shaking his head.

"What a convenient excuse. You always use her to get out of dealing with real problems." He replied sarcastically.

"Real problems? You mean your fragile damaged ass

ego? Because that's all last night was about." I laughed bitterly.

If he wanted to go low, I would go to Hell!

His face darkened, but before he could respond, I grabbed my bag and headed for the door. Fuck this shit!

The car ride was silent, just like I preferred it to be. I stared out the window, counting the streetlights as they passed. I could feel Sam's anger radiating off him, but I didn't give a fuck. I was too consumed by my own turmoil, replaying the video in my mind and trying to figure out what she would do next.

When we arrived at my house, I moved quickly, eager to put space between them. But to my dismay, Sam followed me inside.

"Why are you coming in?" I asked, barely hiding her irritation.

"Because we're not done." He said stubbornly.

I clenched her jaw but said nothing, knowing another argument would only make things worse. Instead, I texted to let her know that she could bring my baby.

Me: I'm home. You can drop Carlie off whenever.

Adara: Okay sweetie. Be there soon.

As I was putting my phone away, I noticed Sam walking towards my bedroom and almost shit myself. It was then that I remembered Jabari's petty ass left the rose right on the bed with his damn nut all over it! Fuck me!

"Wait!" I yelled unintentionally startling Sam.

"Why are you yelling?" He barked making me roll my eyes.

"I think... I uh... I left my charger in your car. Can you go and get it. My phone is going to die soon." I replied hoping that he believed me.

He looked at me suspiciously before he stalked back towards the door.

"Still don't understand why you fucking yelled." He mumbled on his way out with his scary ass.

As soon as the door shut, I sprinted to my bedroom to put the rose away. Sure enough, it was right on the bed sitting as if it was waiting for me. I carefully picked it up and licked my lips as I saw the amount of cum he left on it and in it. The slut in me wanted to lick it, but I refrained. I shook my nasty thoughts away and quickly put the rose back in its designated place.

As soon as I shut the drawer, Sam was walking through my bedroom door empty handed.

"I didn't see a fucking charger, Cassandra." He bitched.
Duh mufucka!

"Oh shit. Maybe it's in my bag at the bottom." I replied while shrugging.

Before he could respond, the sound of a car pulling into the driveway caught our attention. I glanced out the screen door and saw that it was Adara dropping Carlie off. Saved by the fucking bell!

Shortly after, Adara, with a bright smile on her face, led Carlie into the house.

"Mommy!" Carlie squealed, running into my arms.

"Hi, baby! Did you have fun with your favorites?" I asked jokingly while scooping her up and peppering her face with kisses.

"Yes! We played hide and seek, and I won!" Carlie said excitedly.

Adara chuckled.

"She's been a ball of energy all morning. Good luck keeping up." She joked before she handed me Carlie's overnight bag.

"Thanks, Mrs. Drakos. So much!" I said, meaning it.

"No thanks needed. That's our little princess right there. She is welcome anytime. And I mean it. Don't hesitate to call us whenever you need a break." Adara replied sincerely before saying her goodbyes and leaving.

———

As soon as the door closed behind Adara, Carlie was off like a rocket, running into the living room with a burst of energy only an eight-year-old could have.

"Mommy, look! I'm a ballerina!" she cheered, twirling around in a circle.

I smiled, but before I could respond, Sam's voice cut through the moment like a knife.

"Carlie, sit the fuck down somewhere!" He snapped harshly.

Carlie froze mid-twirl, her eyes wide with surprise. Then, her little lip quivered, and tears welled up in her big, brown eyes. I had never yelled at her like that and no one else has either. He had me so fucked up!

"You heard me! Sit your little annoying ass down before I make you!" He added.

"I—I'm sorry," she whispered, her voice trembling before she took off to her room.

The thought of my baby crying because of his bitch ass had me ready to stab him! I ran after my baby to make sure she was okay. I rushed into Carlie's room, shutting the door behind myself. My heart broke as I watched my baby lay in her bed sobbing.

"Don't cry, baby," I whispered, wiping my daughter's tears.

"Did I do something bad?" Carlie asked, her voice small and hesitant.

"No, sweetie. You didn't do anything wrong. He had no right to yell at you." I reassured her.

She nodded, wiping her nose with the back of her hand.

"Is Sam mad at me?" she asked worriedly.

"No, sweetheart. Sam's not mad at you. He's just… having a bad day." I said, hugging her tightly.

Carlie looked up at me, her big red eyes searching mine.

"I don't like him." she said bluntly.

I couldn't help but laugh softly, even as guilt tugged at my chest.

"It's okay, baby. You don't have to like him." I stated honestly.

I comforted her for a little while longer until I felt she was in a better mood.

"I want you to stay in here while I go and talk to Sam, okay? I'll make you a snack too and bring it to you shortly." I informed her.

"Okay Mommy. Thank you." She replied sweetly.

"You are so welcome Princess." I replied before leaving her room.

The second her door closed was the second my anger resurfaced, and I was ready to kill a mufucka. I walked into the living room and had to scoff at this nigga's audacity. The man had his feet kicked up as he watched football as if he hadn't just hurt my damn child. Oh, I had something for that ass!

I grabbed the remote from the coffee table and turned the volume up a bit hoping to drown out my voice.

"I don't give a fuck how mad at me you are, if you ever yell at my child again like that, it will take the Lord himself to pull me off of you!" I barked furiously.

He stood up in annoyance and waved me off as if I was pissing him off and not the other way around.

"She's been running around like a damn maniac since she got here. Someone had to say something." Sam said defensively.

"First of fucking all, she just got here! Secondly, she's a child! She's supposed to run around and play. Lastly, this is HER fucking house. If she wants to walk up the damn walls like Spiderman, she could! What the hell is wrong with you?" I shot back, walking up to face him.

"What's wrong with me? What's wrong with *you*, Cassandra? You let her do whatever she wants, and now she's spoiled. I'm not having that!" he shouted.

I couldn't believe what I was hearing. My hands clenched into fists at my sides as I glared at him.

"Get out," I said, my voice low and trembling with fury.

"What?" He threw his head back and asked incredulously.

"You heard me. Get the fuck out of my house!" I said, pointing toward the door.

"Are you serious right now?" he asked, his face contorting with anger.

"As a muthafuckin heart attack Bitch! You don't get to yell at my daughter and then act like you're in the right.

You've been pissing me off for over 24 hours now. Get your ass out and don't make me say that shit again!" I snapped.

"Fine! But you better hope I still want your ass after all of this! he spat, grabbing his phone off the counter.

I didn't respond, my arms crossed tightly over my chest as I watched him storm out toward the door. As soon as he left, I was going to find the fucking camera in my room. I could care less about Sam's bitch fit!

I watched as he reached to open the door but got the scare of my life when the door was pushed in from the other side, knocking him to the floor.

"Aaah!" I screamed.

Jabari stepped inside and the look on his face scared the shit out of me.

"Jabari... wha..." I began saying but he put his hand up to cut me off.

"I heard you like yelling at little girls. Yell at me bitch ass nigga!" Jabari shouted and my heart stopped.

Oh fuck!

CHAPTER Nine

JABARI

The buzzing of my phone woke me before the sun had fully risen. Groggy and annoyed, I groaned, blindly reaching for it on the nightstand. The screen glowed with an incoming FaceTime call from a familiar name: **Carlie**.

I gave her my number about a month ago when she was at the family house. I had brought Zahra a new doll and didn't know Carlie was there. I felt bad as hell, so I left and went to get her one too. I gave her my number so she could let me know when she was coming over. I never wanted to leave her out again. She immediately called me from her iPad that day, so I was able to save her contact. Me and Carlie have a decent relationship, so her Face Timing me out of the blue wasn't so odd. However, something still set off alarms in my head.

I sat up, running a hand over my face before swiping to answer.

"What's up, Princess?"

Her tear-streaked face appeared on the screen, and I reached to grab my gun from underneath my pillow.

"Jabbie," she whimpered, her small voice cracking.

My jaw clenched.

"What's wrong Princess?" I asked worriedly.

"I don't like Sam! He yelled at me. He said I'm annoying, and I didn't even do anything! And he is yelling at Mommy too!" she said sadly, and it made me want to kill a mufucka.

Every word she spoke twisted the knife deeper into my gut.

"Carlie, listen to me. Where are you right now?" I said while trying to contain my anger.

"In my room," she sniffled, clutching her stuffed animal tightly.

"Stay there. I'll be there soon. Now, when I get there, I need you to stay in your room until either me or your mom tells you its okay to come out. You hear me?" I asked her.

"I hear you." She replied.

Her voice was so tiny and innocent that it made me even more mad. How could anyone call her annoying?

"I need you to promise me that you won't come out. No matter what you hear." I repeated.

I had no clue what I would do when I got there, so I needed her to stay in her room in case shit got really ugly.

"I promise Jabbie." she whispered before hanging up.

I tossed the phone onto the bed, already moving. I spared that hoe ass nigga last night because I really didn't have a reason to whoop his ass. This time, I had all the reasons. I don't give a fuck if Cassie gets mad. And she better not let me find out that he been yelling at Carlie or I'm getting in her shit too!

The drive to Cassie's house was a blur. All I could see was Carlie's tear-streaked face and hear her small, trembling voice. I pulled up the footage from earlier and felt my anger triple listening to him talk to her like that. I turned the feed to LIVE view and heard Cassie going off on his ass. I appreciated that because had she pushed it to the side, I would've been on her ass too. Even so, that still wasn't enough for me.

I'd always had a soft spot for kids. My nieces and nephews know that they can get whatever they want from me. I don't give a fuck what their parents say. Carlie fits in that category too. Just from being around her a handful of times, I could tell she acted just like Cassie, fiery and stubborn but with a softness she tried to hide.

When I pulled up to the house, I hopped out on business. I had my gun in my hand, and I didn't even bother knocking. I didn't even hesitate. Someone was opening the door as I went to reach for the knob and just my luck, it was the man of the hour. I shoved the door open, knocking him down in the process, stepping inside like I owned the place.

I heard Cassie yelp from across the room. I barely gave her ass a glance as I jumped into action. As far as I knew, they both had me and my princess fucked up! I didn't give either of them time to speak.

Sam cursed, clearly caught off guard. "Who the f—"

Before he could finish, I was on his ass... No Diddy.

"I heard you like yelling at little girls. Yell at me bitch ass nigga!" I said before hitting him in the face with the butt of my gun.

"Aaaah! Fuck!" He shouted in agony.

I didn't stop there though. I shut the door behind me and placed my gun on the kitchen counter. Then I walked back over to where he was laying and finished my fucking job.

"Jabari! Stop!" Cassie screamed, but I wasn't hearing none of that shit.

My fist connected with his jaw, and the sound of his bone cracking echoed through the room. The shit was very satisfying if I must say so myself. He tried balling up to protect his face, but I still didn't stop. I grabbed him by the collar, slamming him against the wall.

"You think that shit makes you tough yelling at a fucking child and woman? You think that shit makes you a man? Nigga, you a bitch! Let me show you what a real man looks like." I growled, my face inches from his.

I didn't wait for an answer. My fist found his stomach this time, doubling him over. He tried to swing at me, but he was sloppy and weak as fuck. I dodged it easily, throwing him onto the floor.

"Jabari, please stop!" Cassie's voice cut through my rage, but still, I ignored her.

Sam was on the floor, groaning and trying to crawl away. I crouched down beside him, grabbing a fistful of his shirt to lift his head. His face was already swelling, and one eye was starting to blacken.

"If I find out you raised your voice or even glanced at either of them wrong again, I'll make sure you can't walk away next time." I said, my voice low and deadly.

Sam muttered something incoherent, and I leaned in closer.

"What's that? Got something to say?"

"You're crazy. You think she wants you? You're just some guy she screwed..." he spat, his words slurring.

The words slipped out before I could stop them.

"Yeah, sure did. And she didn't complain, either. I fucked the shit out of her and I'm gonna do it again hoe ass nigga!"

Sam's eyes widened in shock, and I felt a sting of regret. Not for him, but for Cassie. I'm guessing she hadn't told him, and I'd just blown her secret wide the fuck open.

I let him drop back to the floor, standing up and turning to face her.

Her face was a mixture of fury and disbelief. "Get out, Jabari" she said, her voice shaking.

Sam staggered to his feet, clutching his side as he glared at me.

"This isn't over!" he muttered before attempting to walk toward the bathroom near Cassie's kitchen but falling from the pain and groaning loudly.

Cassie slowly walked over and tried to help him but he pushed her away. I started to go after his ass again, but Cassie glared at me so hard she reminded me of Mama Adara. I waited until I heard the door slam before turning back to Cassie.

"You're welcome." I said, my tone dripping with sarcasm.

Her eyes flashed over to me so fast that I thought she would get whiplash.

"What the hell is wrong with you, Jabari?" she barked.

I could tell she was mad as hell, but I don't give a single fuck.

I shrugged.

"Carlie called me and said she needed my help. I handled it."

"You handled it?" she repeated while slightly raising her voice.

"By beating him up? By telling him... You had no right to say that. To tell my fucking business." She said, shaking her head.

"Maybe not. But I'm not sorry." I admitted, stepping closer.

Her breathing picked up

"I know you think you came here to help, but you only just fucked shit up once again. I had already told him to leave! He was leaving! Yet here comes your nugget head ass always wanting to do the most! Leave Jabari! Now!" Cassie barked.

The entire time she spoke, I was staring at her lips. To shut her ass up, I leaned in and attacked her lips with mine. She froze for a moment, and then, to my surprise, she kissed me back. Damn, her lips were so muthafuckin soft.

The kiss was brief, intense, and left us both breathless. Then as if she remembered what was going on, she pushed me away with all of her might. I stepped back, smirking at the mix of emotions on her face.

"I don't know why you keep fooling yourself Mama. Oh and by the way, how did you like the video?" I asked.

The look on her face was fucking hilarious! I knew her little hot ass liked that shit. Cassie was a fucking freak. Her pussy is probably wet right now just from me bringing it up.

She cleared her throat and looked behind her to see where that nigga was before replying.

"Speaking of that, how the fuck do you keep getting in here? And why do you have cameras in my damn house? Is that how you found out what happened? You are fucking crazy and I'm going call the people on your ass!" She snapped lowly.

I laughed and waved her ass off.

"Even you don't believe that. But while you are talking shit, Carlie called me and told me what ole boy said. She wanted me to come save her, so I did. On that note, you can tell my princess the coast is clear. I'll see you later Baby Mama." I sang.

Without another word, I turned and walked out, leaving her standing there fuming.

Later, I found myself at the warehouse, checking on some of the traps from the cameras I'd set up with Zeke. It was our usual routine—making sure everything was running smoothly and tying up loose ends without having to physically be there. But my mind kept drifting back to Cassie.

"You good nigga?" Zeke asked, giving me a sidelong glance.

"Yeah." I lied, adjusting one of the monitors.

He raised an eyebrow.

"You sure? You've been quiet. Your hoe ass is never quiet." He pointed out.

I hesitated, debating whether to tell him about the morning's events. But in the end, I shook my head.

"It's nothing. Just handling some personal shit." I said.

Zeke didn't push, which I appreciated. Instead, we focused on the work, methodically going through our checklist.

But no matter how hard I tried to focus, I couldn't take my mind off the way she'd kissed me back.

Damn, I need some pussy!

I stared at the screen as I replayed the events in my mind. I smiled thinking of how Sam's face looked when I'd hit him, the way Cassie had looked at me, Carlie's voice on the phone. All that shit.

I didn't regret a damn thing.

Cassie might be angry now, but she'd understand eventually. I was never going to let her leave me alone, and Carlie fucked with me tough. All she had to do was get with the fucking program and things would run smoothly. Now if that meant stepping in and playing the villain for a while, so be it.

I'm on whatever the fuck she is on! Wait til she sees what else I have up my sleeve!

CHAPTER Ten

Cassie

The door slammed shut behind Jabari, and I stood frozen in the aftermath. My heart was pounding in my chest, my hands trembling as I tried to calm my hot ass coochie down. Sam startled me as he came stumbling out of the bathroom, clutching his side and wincing in pain. His face was swollen, and one eye was already darkening. Jabari tore his ass up!

"You need to go to the hospital," I said firmly.

On the outside I probably appeared tough and unbothered, but on the inside, I was shitting bricks.

He groaned, leaning against the doorframe for support.

"I don't need or want your help, Cassandra." He spat, though his words were weak.

Ignoring his attitude, I grabbed my phone and dialed my mom. The phone rang twice before she picked up, her warm, familiar voice greeting me.

"Mom, I need you to meet me at the hospital. The one on Spruce." I said quickly.

"What's wrong? Is it Carlie?" She asked worriedly.

"She's fine. But I need you to take her home while I handle something. Can you meet me there?" I assured her, glancing toward Carlie, who was peeking out from her bedroom doorway.

"Of course. I'll leave right now." She replied quickly.

I hung up and turned back to Sam, who looked like he could barely stand.

"Let's get you in the car," I said, moving to his side.

He muttered something under his breath, but I ignored it. Supporting his weight was harder than I expected. He was much heavier than he looked, and he was no help at all. I swear it felt like I was carrying dead weight. By the time we made it to the car, I was out of breath, and my arms were aching.

"Carlie, baby. Come on and hop in. We're going for a ride." I called her as I helped Sam into the passenger seat.

She climbed into the backseat without a word, hugging her stuffed animal tightly. She had gotten a glimpse of Sam, and it probably scared her little ass. Her silence worried me more than anything else. Hoping to ease her fears a bit, I whispered in her ear.

"You little snitch!"

She looked up at me with eyes before giggling lowly. I shook my head with a smirk and hopped in the seat before taking off.

The drive to the hospital felt like it took forever. Sam drifted in and out of consciousness, groaning softly every time the car hit a bump. I won't lie and say that some of those bumps could have been avoided. Oh well.

When we finally arrived, I waved down a nurse, who rushed over with a wheelchair.

"He showed up at my house like this. I don't know what happened to him." I lied as they helped him out of the car.

They nodded, and I couldn't tell from their faces of they believed my lying ass or not. On the way there I made sure to tell Carlie to keep her mouth shut. I hated to tell my baby to lie, but I had to keep this situation under wraps.

I held Carlie's hand tightly as we followed, her little fingers gripping mine like a lifeline. As soon as they took Sam to the back, I sank into one of the waiting room chairs, pulling Carlie onto my lap. My mind raced, and anxiety was beating my ass. I prayed Jabari wouldn't get in trouble for this—not that I'd admit he was involved, but the guilt still fucked with me anyway.

It wasn't long before my mom arrived, looking more concerned than ever. She pulled me into a tight hug, and I felt my resolve weaken for the first time all morning.

"Are you okay?" she asked, brushing my hair out of my face.

"I just need you to take Carlie home. Sam was hurt and I don't know how bad it is. I promise I'll call you when I know more." I said, my voice shaky.

She hesitated, clearly wanting to press for details, but she nodded instead.

"Okay. Come on, Carlie," she said gently, holding out her hand.

Carlie looked at me, her big eyes filled with worry. I knew she was blaming herself since she called Jabari, but

"Mommy, will he be okay?"

"He'll be fine, baby. Go with Grandma, okay? I'll see you soon." I said, forcing a smile.

She nodded reluctantly and followed my mom out of the waiting room.

Not long after, Sam's mother, Samartha, burst into the hospital like a hurricane. Her sharp eyes scanned the room until they landed on me.

"What happened?" she demanded, storming over.

I repeated the same story I'd told the hospital staff.

"He showed up at my house like that. I don't know what happened." I replied with my hands raised.

Her eyes narrowed with skepticism written all over her face.

"And you expect me to believe that?" She snapped.

I met her gaze evenly.

"I honestly don't care what you believe. It's the truth." I snapped back.

She stared at me for a long moment before sighing.

"Fine. But if I find out you're lying—"

"I'm not." I interrupted firmly.

This bitch had me fucked up.

She huffed, crossing her arms.

"We'll see."

When they finally let us into Sam's room, the strain was apparent. He was lying in the hospital bed, his face bruised and battered, and his breathing shallow. I assumed he was sleeping, but his eyes fluttered open when he heard me enter the room.

"Why are you here?" he croaked in disgust.

"Because I care," I said simply, though the words felt dull even to me.

Samartha hovered nearby, watching us like a hawk. When her phone rang, she stepped out of the room to take the call, leaving us alone.

"I think we should end this." I blurted out.

Sam's eyes snapped to mine, fury burning in them.

"You're breaking off our engagement? Because you fucked up?" He asked angrily.

"It's not about that. We've just been arguing too much and it's not healthy for Carlie. Plus, I'm worried about your livelihood—" I said, trying to keep my composure.

Though I wasn't completely happy with Sam, we did have some great moments.

"Don't give me that bullshit! You're doing this because you're guilty. You cheated on me, yet you wanna call it quits! You're lucky I didn't press charges." He snapped.

The accusation hit like a slap, but I kept my composure.

"I'm sorry for what happened. I wish I had a better answer for you, but I truly don't feel good about this. We are just not working." I said quietly.

He glared at me, his hands clenching into fists.

"You're pathetic. You better be worried about that nigga! He seems to have a temper problem. Remember how the last nigga did you?" He spat evilly.

My eyes turned into slits as I tried my best not to cry. How dare he throw my past traumas in my fucking face! Fucking bitch! I should call Jabari here to whoop his ass again! Before I could let his ass know where he could go, the door opened.

I whipped my head to see Samartha walk back in with a bright smile on her face.

"I know this isn't a good time," she began, "but Sam, baby, I'd like you all to meet my new man."

Sam looked at her in disbelief.

"What?" He belted.

"I know the timing couldn't be worse, but we actually had plans before all this happened. I didn't want to flake on him, so I told him to just come up here." She explained.

"Mom... now I don't feel like meeting anyone!" Sam shouted.

She ignored him though. She stepped out into the hallway and returning moments later with her ma... Jabari?!

"Sam, Cassandra... I want you to meet my man, Jason." Samartha proudly said.

I choked on the soda I'd been sipping, coughing violently as the room fell into stunned silence.

"What the hell is this?" Sam shouted, his face turning red.

Samartha looked genuinely confused.

"What's the problem?" She asked.

"He's the reason I'm in here! And His name isn't fucking Jason!" Sam yelled, pointing at Jabari.

Jabari's expression was the picture of innocence. He had the nerve to look confused and hurt.

"I'm sorry. I think you have me mistaken. We've never met before." He said smoothly.

Samartha frowned at her son.

"Maybe you're confused because of your injuries. It seems like someone hit you hard." She suggested.

Sam looked like he was about to cry, and I had to bite the inside of my cheek to keep from laughing.

"I think it's best if everyone leaves." Sam said, his voice shaking.

Jabari placed a hand over his heart, feigning hurt.

"I hope we can meet again on better terms. I hope they find who did this to you." He said before turning to Samartha who stood there glaring at Sam.

Samartha turned her face up, grabbed Jabari's (Jason's) hand, and stormed out of the room without another word. I followed quickly, desperate to avoid any further drama. I had already placed the engagement ring on the bed next to Sam. I've seen and done some messy shit in my life, but this takes the cake!

———

The elevator doors slid shut, and I found myself stuck on there with Jabari and Samartha. I should've just gone for the stairs, but my fat ass in not in shape for that. Plus, the quicker I can get to my car, the sooner I can leave this circus.

He stood close to her, his hand on the small of her back, whispering something that made her giggle. I stared straight ahead, doing my best to ignore them, but the sight made my stomach churn. I don't see how he was even able to keep a straight face. Samartha is uglier than ten ugly bitches!

When the elevator finally stopped, I practically sprinted out, heading straight for my car.

"Cassie!" Samartha called after me. "We should do dinner together—like a double date!"

I pretended not to hear her, climbing into my car and slamming the door shut. I saw the two of them hug before she turned to walk back inside the hospital. What tickled me the most was how she was trying to switch them fragile ass hips. Knowing she has the ass of brick wall.

The moment I pulled out of the hospital, the laughter burst out of me. I laughed so hard that tears streamed down my face. This was the most absurd shit I have ever experienced.

———

I was almost home when my phone buzzed, and I glanced at the screen to see Jabari's name. I hesitated but answered anyway.

"Hey Jason!" I said sarcastically.

He was laughing so hard that it took him a moment to speak.

"Don't tell me you're jealous Mama? You know I didn't give that old bitch this dick. That's all for you!" He replied playfully.

"You're sick. How did you even pull some shit off like that?" I asked, trying not to laugh.

"You don't even want to know." he replied, still laughing.

"You may be right. I don't want to know," I said, shaking my head.

"Well, I'll never reveal my secrets. Just know I got some

more shit up my sleeves. Just wait on it. Until then, I just texted you my address. Pull up on yo boy." he said.

I hesitated, weighing my options. Then, with a sigh, I said, "Why not?"

———

When I arrived at his house, my intention was to confront him, to get answers about the cameras and the chaos he'd just caused. But as soon as I stepped inside, all my defenses melted away. His eyes met mine, and the magnetic pull between us was fucking dangerous.

Before either of us could take a step, the cutest cat I had ever seen came rubbing against my leg. I cooed as I bent down to pet it.

"Aren't you the cutest little thing!" I sang.

"Yeah, that's my lil nigga right there, Tiger." Jabari called out.

It took me a second to realize what he said before I started cracking the fuck up.

"Wait, this is the Tiger that you were going to feed Sam to?" I asked in tears.

"You damn right! Don't let that cute face fool you! My lil nigga gets busy!" Jabari replied only making it funnier.

"I fucking cannot with you!"

Without a word, he closed the distance between us, his hands finding my waist as he pulled me close. He nudged Tiger away and lifted my chin to look at him.

I didn't resist.

"Fuck all that. Come put that pussy on my face."

"Shiiit. Lead the way!" I replied.

Fuck it! I'm single now!

CHAPTER Eleven

Jabari

"Why you acting like you knew to this? Ride my fucking face!" I barked before slapping her thick ass thigh.

"Shit! Okay! Wait!" Cassie cried out.

I was currently laying on my bed with her hovering over my face. Her pussy was so wet that the shit dripped onto my face before she even sat down. I don't know why her ass is acting brand new like she's never been in this position before, but I'm about to show her ass.

I wrapped my arms around her thighs and smushed her pussy all over my face. I swear her shit was in my mouth, nose, and eyes. I didn't give a fuck. When I say ride my face, that's what the fuck I mean!

"Bariiiii! Shiiiiit! You so fucking nastyyyy!" She screamed.

Slurping and sucking sounds were all that was heard underneath her loud ass moans. I needed her to cum at least once more before I gave her this dick.

"Babyyy! I'm cumming!" She shouted.

Then she began bucking hard against my face making me groan. That's what the fuck I'm talking about!

"Ahhhhhhh! You muthafucka!" She cried out.

Before she could get herself together, I flipped her off of my head. Hell, I was starting to get lightheaded anyways. She lay on her back with her legs wide open staring at me. Her pussy lips were so fat that you could barely see her clit. And the juices that ran down her ass onto my bed had me damn near nutting.

I stroked my dick and watched as she spread her pussy lips and rubbed her clit in a circular motion.

"Did I tell you to touch my pussy?" I asked tauntingly.

"I can... I can't help itttt." She moaned.

"Move your fucking hand!" I shouted.

She reluctantly obliged and I could see the desperation in her eyes. She was about to cum again. I began rubbing my dick against her folds roughly to cause some friction. As soon as it slipped between them lips and rubbed that clit, it was over.

"I'm cumming again! What the fuck!" She screamed.

I quickly shoved my dick right inside of her making her eyes buck and her voice get caught in her throat.

"Ah! Breathe Mama! Breathe!" I cooed.

I watched as she came apart. Her nut was so strong that it damn near pushed my dick out of her.

"I can't take it! I can't!" She cried.

Now why would she say that? I placed my hand on her lower belly to keep her still, and started fucking the shit out of her. My balls slapped against her fat ass and I could feel my nut rising.

"Shit! Whyyyy?" She groaned.

"Why what Mama?" I grunted as I kept pumping away.

"Why are you fucking me like thissss?" She replied while pulling at her hair.

I loved to see her lose control. She needed to know who the fuck to play with.

"I'm fucking you too good Mama? Huh? You want Daddy to stop?" I asked teasingly.

"I wish you fucking would!" She snapped making me smirk.

"Shit, I'm about to bust. Grab that rose from under that pillow. I want you to use that mufucka while I fuck you." I instructed.

She frowned at me before slowly reaching where I told her to.

"This better not... FUCK... be used by no other... Ooohhh... bitch!" She snapped while still panting.

I was tearing her shit up and she still found time to talk shit.

"That's actually your shit. I stopped and grabbed it from your crib on the way here." I informed her.

Her mouth dropped in shock and before she could question me, I snatched the rose from her hand and turned it on. As soon as it touched her clit, she started squirming all over the place. I grabbed her hand to replace mine on the rose, then grabbed her by the throat.

I began slow stroking her, hard and deep as I leaned down and stuck my tongue in her mouth. Her greedy ass inhaled my tongue. Sucking on it as if was her favorite popsicle.

"Mmmmmm!" She moaned.

"I know Mama. I feel ittttt. Wet my shit up." I coached her.

Within seconds, we were cumming together. I moaned into her mouth and damn near shed a tear at how tight her pussy was squeezing me.

"Fuck girl! Let my shit go!" I groaned.

She started rolling her hips underneath me and I had to bite my lip to not cry out like a bitch.

"Cassie. If you don't want another round, I suggest you chill the fuck out. My lil nigga wake back up, you gone have to put him to sleep." I threatened.

She smacked her lips before giggling.

"Ain't shit little about that damn tree trunk you call a dick! You done stretched my girl all out!" She sassed.

I slid out of her slowly and smirked as my dick flopped out. She wasn't lying. My dick measured around 9 inches long and 6 inches in girth. My shit is heavy, and I can work this mufucka. That's the real reason she been ducking a nigga. She's trying not to get stuck on stupid bout a nigga.

―――

The room was quiet except for the sound of our breathing slowly evening out. Cassie lay beside me, her soft and warm body lay snuggled next to mine, her hair was a sexy mess scattered all over my pillow. I traced lazy patterns on her back, watching her eyes flutter closed.

"Don't fall asleep." I teased, brushing my lips against her temple.

"I'm not." she murmured, though her voice was laced

with the kind of exhaustion that only came from being thoroughly dicked down.

I smirked, pressing a kiss to her bare shoulder.

"Come on, let's clean up before you knock out on me."

She groaned but sat up, grabbing the sheet to wrap around herself as if I hadn't just seen every inch of her. "What time is it?"

"Time to wash yo ass nigga." I said, sliding out of bed and holding out my hand.

She hesitated for a second before taking it, and I led her into the bathroom. Steam was already starting to fill the space by the time we stepped under the water.

At first, the shower was calm and simply just relaxing. Cassie tilted her head back, letting the water cascade over her hair and down her back, and I found myself staring. The curve of her neck, the arch of her back—it was like she was designed to drive me fucking crazy.

"Enjoying the view?" she asked, catching me staring.

"Absolutely." I replied without hesitation.

She rolled her eyes, but her lips twitched in a half-smile. I stepped closer, the water streaming between us, and cuffed her titties in my hands. I loved touching her thick ass. She had stretch marks on each of her hips that made me want to lick them muthafuckas. It was so sexy to me. She carried a whole child and still has the nerve to walk around with a vice grip pussy.

"Jabari, we just—"

"I know, but you're kind of fucking irresistible." I interrupted, smirking.

Her laugh was cut off as my lips found hers, the water cascading around us like we were in our own little world.

Her hands slid up my chest, her nails grazing my skin making me groan.

By the time we stumbled out of the shower, the bathroom mirror was completely fogged, and we were both out of breath again. Cassie wrapped herself in one of my towels, her cheeks flushed, and gave me a playful glare.

"You're insatiable," she muttered.

"Only when it comes to you." I shot back, grabbing another towel to dry off.

She shook her head, but I caught the small smile on her lips before she turned away.

Back in the bedroom, I tossed on a pair of sweatpants while Cassie borrowed one of my shirts, which looked way too good on her.

"I'm starving," she announced, flopping onto my bed like she hadn't just eaten me alive in the shower.

I'm going to change her name in my phone to Dyson. Man, the way she sucked my dick should be illegal!

"I'll order something. What do you have a taste for?" I asked, grabbing my phone.

"Anything but pizza." she said, scrolling through her own phone.

"Got it." I said, placing the order for Chinese food.

After confirming it'd be about thirty minutes, I grabbed my controller and turned on my gaming setup.

"You're really about to play video games right now?" she asked, arching an eyebrow.

"Why not? Food's not here yet. I mean, unless you

tryna give me some more pussy..." I suggested while wiggling my eyebrows.

She rolled her eyes but moved to sit on the couch in the corner of my room, pulling her legs up under her.

Zeke's annoying ass voice came through my speakers as I logged in.

"Finally, mufucka! I was starting to think you got lost on the way to your own console." he bitched.

"Relax Bitch. I'm here now. Let's run it." I shot back, grinning as I adjusted my headset.

Cassie chuckled from the couch, and I glanced over to see her shaking her head.

"You two sound like teenagers." she said, laughing as Zeke yelled something about me stealing his kill.

"Tell her to mind her business." Zeke's voice came through the speakers, loud enough for her to hear.

"I can hear you, Zeke!" she called out, laughing.

"Good! Mind your damn business, Cassie!" He repeated making us laugh.

We played for the next twenty minutes, and the shit talking between me and Zeke kept Cassie entertained. She was laughing so hard at one point that she had tears in her eyes, clutching her stomach as Zeke and I argued over a near-loss.

When the doorbell rang, I tossed my controller on the desk and went to grab the food. Cassie followed me to the kitchen, her laughter finally dying down as I set the bags on the counter.

"Smells good," she said, grabbing plates from the cabinet like she lived here.

I watched her move around the kitchen, and my chest tightened in a way I didn't like. She fit too well into my space, like she belonged here. Like she belonged to me. That's too fucking much.

———

We sat on the couch, eating in comfortable silence for a while. But I could feel her stealing glances at me, like she was working up the courage to say something.

Finally, she set her plate down and looked at me. "What do you want from me, Jabari?"

Her question caught me off guard, but I kept my expression neutral. "What do you mean?"

"I mean... this." She gestured between us. "What are we doing? What do you want from me?"

I leaned back, running a hand over my jaw.

"Honestly, I don't want shit." I said after a moment.

Her eyebrows shot up.

"Nothing?" She asked.

"Nothing. I thought we were just vibing. I'm not trying to be in a relationship, Cassie." I repeated.

Her lips pressed into a thin line, but I kept going.

"But I also don't want you fucking with anyone else. We can just fuck each other." I finished.

That did it. Her eyes narrowed, and she set her plate on the coffee table with a clatter.

"Are you fucking serious?" She barked.

"What?" I asked, already knowing I'd messed up.

"You don't want a relationship, but you don't want me to be with anyone else? Do you even hear yourself, Jabari?"

I stayed quiet, knowing anything I said would only make it worse.

"That's the most childish shit I've ever heard. You need to grow the fuck up!" she snapped, standing up.

I opened my mouth to respond, but the words wouldn't come. She was right, and I hated the shit.

Cassie stormed to the bedroom, pulling on her clothes with quick, angry movements.

"I'm done, Jabari. When I leave this house, do not call me, text me, break in my fucking house, or plant no more fucking cameras." she said as she slipped on her shoes.

I wanted to stop her, to say something that would fix this, but my feet wouldn't move.

"I got the best fucking luck with men don't I?" She muttered to herself with a scoff.

"One beat my ass for breakfast lunch and dinner, the other is a bitch ass mama's boy, and now this nigga scared to commit but wanna be a fucking peeping Tom ass fuck boy. Ugh! I swear I am done!" She continued expressing out loud.

Again, I said nothing.

She grabbed her bag and headed for the door.

And... I let her go.

The sound of the door closing echoed in the quiet room. I sat there for a while, staring at the spot where she'd been. What a fucking turn of events!

My phone buzzed on the coffee table, and I picked it up to see a message from Zeke.

Zeke: *Fuck happened to you nigga?*

I didn't even bother to reply. I put the food away and went to get in my damn bed. I had lost my fucking appetite.

———

All night, I lay in bed replaying her words over and over. She was right—I was a childish ass nigga. But it didn't matter, because I didn't know how to be anything else.

And the worst part? I couldn't stop thinking about her ass.

CHAPTER Twelve

Cassie

The past couple of weeks had been surprisingly peaceful. It felt strange, almost unnatural, to exist in a world without the weight of Sam and his ugly ass mama dragging me down. I thought I'd miss him, but the truth was, I didn't. If anything, I felt lighter—freer.

Carlie and I had settled into a rhythm, just the two of us. Mornings were filled with laughter as we rushed through breakfast and got ready for our days. Evenings were cozy, spent curled up on the couch watching movies or working on her homework together. And in the quiet moments when she was asleep, I focused on building the life I wanted for us.

My business proposal was finally coming together. I could almost see the spa now: soft music, calming scents, and women leaving feeling as beautiful as they were. It was a dream I'd held onto for so long, and for the first time, it felt tangible.

Of course, there were moments when my thoughts drifted to Jabari. His touch, his voice, the way he looked at me like I was the only person in the room. But I pushed those thoughts away every time they crept in. I couldn't afford to get lost in him—not again.

I'd even changed the locks at the house. I never even gave his ass a key in the first fucking place. The same night I left his house, I went home and swept my entire house from top to bottom. I found 6 fucking hidden cameras and even saw that his psychotic ass had my location on his phone. I did his ass one better and got a whole new phone and number. It was my way to reclaim my space and my peace.

———

I stared at the box sitting on my passenger seat. It was full of Sam's things: a couple of sweatshirts, some books, and the watch I'd gotten him for his birthday. It wasn't much, but it felt heavy all the same.

Pulling up to his house, I took a deep breath before grabbing the box and heading to the door. I didn't bother knocking... Sam had already seen me through the window and opened it before I could even reach the steps.

"Well, look who it is." he said, leaning against the doorframe with a smug look on his face.

"Here. That's everything." I said, shoving the box into his arms.

"Gee, thanks." he muttered, setting the box inside.

"I'll grab my things now." I said, stepping past him before he could say anything else.

His mom was sitting on the couch, her lips pursed in disapproval as soon as she saw me.

"Back to cause more problems, I see." she said, folding her arms.

"I'm just here to get my things," I replied irritably.

"You've already taken enough from him. Maybe you should leave what little he has left alone." she snapped.

I turned to her, feeling my patience snap.

"Listen, Samartha, your son and I are done. That's it. I don't want shit from him except what belongs to me. So, unless you want to add to the list of reasons why he's single, and will probably stay single, I suggest you mind your fucking business for the first time in your miserable ass life." I snapped.

She gasped, but I didn't give her a chance to respond. I grabbed my things from the corner where Sam had thrown them and headed for the door.

"Good riddance." Sam muttered as I walked past him.

I stopped, turning to face him.

"You know what, Sam? You're so muthafuckin pathetic. You'll never find someone who puts up with your nonsense the way I did. Or fake being satisfied from that mediocre ass dick you used to give. Why do you think I cheated in the first place? Keep fucking with me and I'll hurt your bitch ass feelings!" I shouted.

And with that, I walked out, slamming the door behind me.

By the time I got to Genesis and Kenzo's house, my mood had shifted. Seeing her standing at the door with a warm smile and a glass of wine in her hand felt like a reset button.

"Hey, girl." she said, letting me in.

"Kenzi and Carlie are already in the backyard, and KJ is terrorizing his aunt Pilar." She informed me.

I laughed, handing her the small bag of snacks I'd brought. I had my mom drop Carlie off to Genesis early this morning so I wouldn't have to make an extra trip. Plus, I still hadn't really explained to her what happened between Sam and I. So, I was avoiding her for a minute.

"Perfect. I need this today." I expressed.

We made our way to the living room, where Pilar was sitting on the floor with Kenzo Jr. trying to keep him from crawling under the couch. Her twin boys, Ameer and Xavier, were in the playpen nearby, babbling to each other in their own little language.

"Cassie! Come save me from your godson. He's a damn menace like his father." Pilar called out, looking up with a grin.

I laughed, scooping up KJ and settling him on my hip. "He's not bad! He is just curious."

"Curious about destruction." Pilar muttered, standing up and dusting off her leggings.

Once the kids were settled with toys and snacks, the three of us sat down on the couch. Genesis poured us glasses of wine, and I let out a long sigh as I took a sip.

"Rough day?" she asked.

"Rough couple of weeks." I admitted.

I told them everything—about Sam, his mom, and the way I felt like I was finally free of them both. Then, somehow, the conversation shifted to Jabari.

"I don't even know why I let him get under my skin like that." I said, swirling the wine in my glass.

"Because he's Jabari. He has a way of making you feel like you're the center of his world. That's until he gets scared, and he decides he's not ready to give you that spot or commit." Pilar said with a shrug.

Genesis nodded in agreement.

"He's always been like that. Intense, but guarded. It's frustrating. He acts so tough like he doesn't need anyone but is really a big ass baby."

"It's exhausting. I just want to know where I stand, but every time I think I have him figured out, he pulls away." I corrected.

Pilar leaned forward, her expression softening. "Cassie, listen. Jabari is complicated, but he cares about you. I know he does. That being said, you have to decide if his version of caring is enough for you."

Genesis chimed in, "And don't let him take up space in your life if he's not willing to meet you halfway. You deserve more than that."

I nodded, their words sinking in. They were right—I knew they were. But knowing didn't make it any easier.

———

We spent the rest of the afternoon talking and laughing. We knew the kids were also having fun because we could hear their laughter echoing from the backyard. For the first time in a while, I felt like I could breathe again.

As I helped clean up Pilar get the boys ready so she could leave, Genesis gave me a tight hug.

"Whatever you decide, just know we've got your back," she said.

"Always," Pilar added, giving me a reassuring smile.

I smiled back, feeling a little lighter than I had been feeling for a while now. Maybe I didn't have all the answers yet, but for now, I had something better... hope.

CHAPTER Thirteen

Jabari

I sat in my car for what felt like hours, parked outside the family house. This place had been my sanctuary since I was a kid, the one constant thing in my life that had been anything but stable. Yet, as I sat there staring at the driveway, a knot twisted in my stomach.

I wasn't sure what I was looking for in coming here. Answers, maybe. Guidance, definitely. All I knew was that my mind was a mess, and I needed to clear it. This shit was stressing out and weed wasn't even helping.

That heffa Cassie had been consuming my thoughts. The memory of her leaving my house that night was like a sad ass love song stuck on repeat. The shit she said to me, the fire in her eyes, the way I wanted to chase after her but didn't. She had every right to walk away. Hell, I'd all but shoved her out the door with my stubbornness and fucked up mentality.

But I couldn't stop thinking about her. And that scared

me and annoyed the fuck out of me at the same damn time.

Finally, I got out of the car and headed inside. The familiar scent of Mama's cooking hit me as soon as I opened the door. The shit reminded me of my childhood.

"Jabari! You better get in here before I come drag you in myself. I saw you pull up and been waiting on your butt to come inside!" Mama's voice floated from the kitchen.

A small smile tugged at my lips as I made my way to the kitchen. She stood at the stove, stirring something in a pot that smelled heavenly. Her long hair was tied back, and her face lit up when she saw me.

"Hey, Mama." I said, leaning down to kiss her cheek.

She swatted me playfully with a wooden spoon. "Don't 'hey, Mama' me. You've been avoiding me for weeks. Sit down and tell me what's going on with my baby."

Before I could respond, Sayid walked in, his presence filling the room like it always did. He looked as sharp as ever, even in a simple button-down and slacks.

"Jabari. What's this? A visit without a summons?" he said sarcastically.

I chuckled, sitting at the table as he joined me. "Something like that."

Mama placed a plate of food in front of me without asking if I was hungry. She knew me too well to bother.

"Eat while you talk." she said, sitting across from me.

I hesitated, unsure how to start. Sayid leaned back in his chair, studying me with that piercing gaze of his.

"Spit it out, boy. What's eating you?" he asked.

I sighed, running a hand over my face. "It's Cassie."

Mama's expression softened immediately, while Sayid's brow furrowed slightly.

"I don't know what to do. She's different. No matter how hard I try to push her out of my mind, she's still there. But I'm not built for relationships. I don't want to get hurt, and I don't want to hurt her either. It's easier to just...keep my distance." I admitted.

Sayid rubbed his chin thoughtfully.

You're scared. And that's fine. But the question is, are you more scared of getting hurt or of losing her?" he said plainly.

The weight of his words hit me like a punch to the gut.

"I don't know," I said honestly.

Sayid leaned forward, his voice lowering.

"Let me tell you something about your father, Jayson. He was just as stubborn as you. Thought he didn't need anyone. But when he met your mother? Everything changed. He knew she was it for him, and he was willing to risk everything to keep her."

He paused, his gaze intense. "That's how I felt about Adara. From the moment I saw her, I knew she was worth it. Worth the risk of getting hurt, worth the sleepless nights, worth it all. Because losing her wasn't an option."

Mama reached over, placing a hand on his arm. The love between them was one of a kind, and for a moment, I envied it.

Sayid turned back to me. "So, you tell me, Jabari. Is Cassie worth the risk?"

I opened my mouth to respond, but Mama held up a hand, stopping me.

"Before you answer that, let me say this," she said.

"Women like Cassie don't wait around forever. She's strong, yes, but strength has its limits. If you keep hurting her, disappointing her, eventually she'll walk away for good."

Her words stung because I knew they were true.

"Sex won't fix it," she continued.

"It might patch things up temporarily, but it won't solve the real problem. If you're not ready to give her what she deserves—a commitment, honesty, love—then you need to let her go. Completely. Don't keep her in limbo because you're scared."

I stared down at my plate, as all of their advice settled on my shoulders. Fuck man. I should've never came here.

After I left the house, my mind was still a storm of confusion. I drove aimlessly for a while before pulling into a corner store. If nothing else, a bottle of Remy might help me quiet my thoughts.

I grabbed the bottle, paid the clerk, and stepped back outside. The night air was cool, and it was refreshing. Inside I was burning the fuck up.

As I walked to my car, I heard footsteps behind me. Before I could react, I felt the cold press of a gun against my back.

"Give me everything you got! Now! And don't try nothing stupid!" a voice growled.

I cursed under my breath, reaching for my pocket. But as I handed over my wallet, the guy's partner snatched the bottle from my other hand.

"Nice try." he sneered.

The next thing I knew, pain exploded in my side as a gunshot rang out. I collapsed to the ground, clutching my abdomen. They opened the doors to my car and started searching through it. I'm assuming they didn't find what they were looking for because I could hear them cursing.

"Fuck it, Nigga! Let's go before someone calls the pigs!" One of them snapped.

They ran off, and I could hear them fussing in the distance. Dumb ass niggas didn't even take my whip or my phone. I fumbled for my phone, my vision blurring as blood soaked my shirt.

"Zeke, I got shot bro. I'm... fuck." I mumbled when he answered.

"Fuck you just say?! Jabari? Where are you? Shit!" He yelled.

I barely managed to give him the location before darkness closed in.

CHAPTER Fourteen

Cassie

Genesis's laugh echoed through the living room as I recounted one of my more ridiculous encounters with an annoying ass client. Pilar had left a few hours ago, and it was just me, Genesis, and the kids now. We had Pandora playing all of the old school jams in the background and this wine had me feeling myself.

"It sounds like you handled it better than I would have. I would've told that bitch to fins another spa to go to!" Genesis said, shaking her head.

"Listen I wanted to so damn bad, but I don't discriminate against the money. I'm collecting every dollar until I can get my spot." I said, leaning back on the couch.

We both laughed, the kind of laugh that felt like a release, a reminder that life could still be simple and good.

Then Genesis's phone rang, cutting through the lighthearted moment. She glanced at the screen and frowned. "It's Pilar."

"Answer it." I said, sensing the shift in her demeanor.

She put the call on speaker. "Hey, Pilar, what's up?"

The sound of Pilar sobbing was the first thing we heard. My stomach dropped.

"Genesis! They shot my fucking brother! My baby! He got fucking robbed!" Pilar's voice cracked.

The words hit me like a kangaroo kick to the chest.

"What? What happened? Where is he? I she going to be okay?" Genesis shouted, standing up so fast that her chair nearly tipped over.

"He's at the house," Pilar managed between sobs.

"Doctors are with him now. They said the bullet went straight through, but—" She broke off, her voice trembling. "He's my baby brother, Genesis. I can't... I can't lose him."

I froze. Jabari? Shot? No! No the fuck he didn't.

The room started to spin, and I had to grip the edge of the couch to steady myself. Images of him flashed in my mind—his smirk, his laugh, the way he looked at me like I was the only person in the world who mattered.

"Cassie. We have to get the kids ready and go. Are you going to be okay?" Genesis said, snapping me out of my daze.

"I...I don't know." I admitted, my voice barely above a whisper.

Genesis reached for my hand, her grip firm and grounding.

"He's going to be okay." she said, more to herself than to me. "He has to be."

The drive to the Drakos estate felt like an eternity. Genesis's husband, Kenzo, had called her while we were on the way, confirming that Jabari was stable but still in critical condition.

When we arrived, the house was quiet aside from the sobs coming from Pilar. Adara stood in the grand foyer, her usually composed demeanor replaced with a raw, frantic energy.

"Where is he?" Genesis asked, rushing to her mother-in-law.

Adara's eyes were red, but her voice was steady. "Upstairs. The doctors are still with him."

I hesitated at the base of the stairs, unsure if I should follow. This wasn't my family. Did I even have a right to be here?

Adara turned to me, her gaze softening. "Go," she said, as if reading my thoughts. "He needs you."

Her words broke something in me. I nodded and followed Genesis upstairs.

The door to the room was slightly ajar, and I caught a glimpse of Jabari lying on the bed, pale but alive. A doctor stood over him, checking the wound on his side while another checked his vitals.

I stayed just outside the door, my heart pounding in my chest. Seeing him like that—so vulnerable—made me nauseous. I was literally sick to my fucking stomach.

"Cassie," a voice called softly.

I turned to see Pilar, her face streaked with tears. She pulled me into a tight hug, her body trembling against mine.

"He's strong. He will pull through." she said, as if trying to convince herself.

I nodded, unable to find my voice.

After what felt like hours, the doctors finally left the room, giving the all-clear for visitors. Mr. And Mrs. Drakos went in first and Mr. Drakos had to damn near carry her out of the room. Their relationship was so loving. I knew she was hurting.

The brothers went in after and from the looks on their faces, someone or some people were going die painfully and slowly. Pilar and Genesis went in, and Adonis had to come and get Pilar. She broke down again and he couldn't take it. I stayed back, giving everyone their moment.

When Genesis finally stepped out, she placed a hand on my shoulder. "He's asking for you."

I walked into the room, my legs feeling like they might give out at any moment. Jabari's eyes were closed, but when I approached the bed, they fluttered open.

"Hey. You came." he said, his voice hoarse but still carrying that familiar teasing lilt.

Tears blurred my vision as I sat down beside him. "Of course I'm here, you fucking idiot. You scared the shit out of me."

He managed a weak smile. "I ain't ask them niggas to pop me."

The dam broke, and I started crying, my shoulders shaking with the force of it.

"I thought I was going to lose you." I admitted, my voice cracking.

Jabari reached out, his hand brushing against mine. "Hey," he said softly. "Calm down. I'm still here."

I leaned down, pressing a kiss to his forehead. His skin was warm, and that made me feel a lot better. He looked cold and dead earlier.

"I care about you. More than I fucking should and I hate it." I said.

The words spilled out before I could stop them.

Jabari chuckled, wincing slightly. "You're making me sound like a burden."

"You are. But you're my burden." I shot back.

I probably looked crazy as hell crying over a nigga that ain't mine, but I don't even care right now.

He reached up, cupping my face with a tenderness that took my breath away.

"I'm glad you're here." he admitted, his voice quieter now. "I was hoping you'd come."

I kissed him again, this time on the lips, pouring every ounce of fear, relief, and love into it.

As I pulled back, Jabari smirked, though it was clear he was exhausted.

"You're staying, right?" he asked, and I could see the worry in his eyes.

"Of course." I said without hesitation.

"I'll have someone get the guest room ready for Carlie." he said.

"Just for her? What about me?" I asked, already knowing the answer.

"Just for her. You're staying with me." He replied.

My cheeks flushed, but I didn't argue. I knew this situation wouldn't change much between us, but I would enjoy it for the time being.

As Jabari's breathing evened out and his eyes began to close, I whispered a silent prayer...

"Thank you for saving him."

CHAPTER Fifteen

Jabari

THE FIRST THING I noticed when I woke up was the ache radiating through my side. Painkillers or not, the shit hurt like a muthafucka and made me instantly remember what happened to me. Hoe ass niggas! The second thing I noticed was Cassie, curled up in the chair beside my bed. Her head rested on her folded arms and her cute snores had me grinning like a lil bitch.

She was here.

Suddenly, a memory of her hovering over me last night, praying and crying, played in my head. It wasn't often that someone prayed or cried for me like that. Like they couldn't bear the thought of losing me. That shit touched me.

I'm tripped out on how the fuck me and my sister get shot in the same damn spot? This shit was not on my fucking bingo card! I shifted slightly, wincing as pain shot through my side. The movement must've woken her because her head shot up, her eyes immediately locking onto mine.

"Jabari. You're awake." she said softly.

Her voice was laced with so much relief it was as if she had been holding her breath the entire time.

"Barely. Feels like I got hit by a damn truck." I muttered, attempting to adjust myself.

Cassie leaned forward, brushing her hands against mine.

"Why are you trying to get up? You need to rest. You were shot, for God's sake." She bitched.

"I'm fine." I said, though my body disagreed.

Her eyebrows furrowed, and she gave me that look. You know, the one that said she wasn't buying a word of what I was saying.

"You're not fine. You're lucky to be alive, Jabari. You need to take it easy." she said firmly.

Before I could argue, she stood up.

"How about I make you some breakfast." she suggested.

I raised an eyebrow.

"In my mama's kitchen?"

Cassie hesitated, chewing on her bottom lip. "You think she'd mind?"

"Nah. But you better text her first. She runs that kitchen like it's her kingdom." I said with a smirk.

Cassie pulled out her phone, quickly typing a message. She glanced back at me. "Don't try to get out that damn bed, Jabari." she snapped.

"Yes, ma'am." I said teasingly.

She rolled her eyes but smiled as she left the room.

As soon as the door closed, the grin fell from my face. I

can't believe that after all my years of living recklessly, I got caught slipping. A mufucka really had the audacity to pop me! One of the most thorough niggas in Philly! And they didn't stick around to make sure I was dead.

I was alive.

The bullet had gone clean through, missing anything vital. The doctor said it was pure luck. But luck didn't explain the pit in my stomach or the tightness in my chest.

I could've fucking died.

The thought settled over me like a heavy weight. If the bullet had been an inch to the left, I wouldn't be here. I wouldn't have woken up to Cassie by my side, or to my family downstairs. My mama would've been sick, and my brothers would have fucked Philly up.

I rubbed a hand over my face, trying to push the thoughts away. But the only thing that kept coming to me was revenge and how soon I would get it.

———

By the time I managed to sit up in bed, I could hear faint voices coming towards my room. They began laughing at something and I immediately knew it was Cassie and my mama. Two people who hold a strong and permanent spot in my life. Cassie just didn't know it yet.

Adara Drakos was a force to be reckoned with. She had taken me and Pilar in when we were just kids, showing us more love and care than we had ever known outside of our dad. She wasn't just my adoptive mother—she was my anchor.

Cassie's voice carried a nervous edge, but my mama's

laugh broke through, giving her the warmth that she gave everyone she came in contact with.

A few seconds later, the door opened and the smell of bacon and something sweet had my stomach doing backflips. My stomach growled, and I couldn't wait to fuck some shit up. I looked at my mama and I knew she was about to start her crying mess.

"Cry later old lady, I'm hungry!" I joked.

"Kiss my ass Jabari!" She replied playfully.

———

The dining room was loud as hell by the time Cassie and Mama brought the food out. My brothers, their wives, and the kids had all shown up. They scared the shit out of me when they burst into my room to check on me. It shocked me that they left at all. They made sure to pull up early as hell though. I swear the table looked like the dinner scene from *Home Alone.*

I wheeled myself into the room, immediately catching Cassie's eye. She was setting a plate down in front of an empty spot that I assumed was for me. The way she frowned when she saw me down here had me cracking up. This girl was going to be hell!

"You should've let someone help you! I was on my way up!" she snapped, walking over to me.

"It was nothing. I'm good." I said, brushing off her concern.

She sighed, but the small smile on her lips let me know that she wasn't that mad. "Stubborn as ever." she mumbled.

"Been that way his entire life unfortunately." Pilar added.

I stuck my middle finger up at her and rubbed my hands together ready to get the fuck down on that plate. My shit was stacked up with eggs, bacon, pancakes, potatoes, and fruit. Cassie and Mama had outdone themselves.

"These potatoes are slamming! You wait til this nigga gets shot to start adding food to the menu?" Kenzo asked playfully with his arm slung casually around Genesis's chair.

"They taste like Mommy's potatoes!" Carlie said happily from the kid's table.

Mama laughed. "That's because they are. While you talking shit Kenzo. Cassie made them. Hell, she made the most of it. I just supervised."

My eyebrows raised in surprise. I stuck my fork in the potatoes and had to see what they were hitting on. As soon as them bitches hit my tongue, I had to close my eyes. She seasoned them potatoes with her all. I had to look at her and nod my head. I couldn't even speak cuz I was fucking that food up.

Cassie blushed under everyone's praise, but I could see the pride in her eyes.

As we ate, the conversation flowed easily, filled with laughter and stories. But beneath it all, I could feel the tension. Everyone was worried about me, even if they didn't say it outright.

"I can't believe they've got me in this damn wheelchair," I muttered, pushing a piece of pancake around my plate.

Cassie shot me a look. "It's only temporary."

"Still feels like I'm a hundred years old," I grumbled.

The table erupted in laughter, and I couldn't help but laugh with them. This some bullshit.

After breakfast, the mood shifted. My brothers and I gathered in my room upstairs and got to business. All the playful shit from earlier was gone. Now, I needed to find me a few mufuckas that's eager to die.

"We've got surveillance from the street cameras. The quality is trash, and from what I see, them are some random ass niggas. It's only a matter of time before we figure out who they are." Zeke said, leaning against the desk.

"And then what? We wait? I could be putting my ear to the streets and shaking a few mufuckas up at least." I said angrily.

Kenzo shook his head. "We will handle it. Until then, you are not hitting the streets until you're healed. They didn't fuck you up badly, but you still got shot nigga."

I clenched my fists in frustration. I wasn't trying to hear that shit at all. "I can't just sit here while mufuckas out there thinking they got one over on me."

Adonis stepped forward with anger all over his face. "You almost died, Baby Bro. Let us handle this."

"I'm not fucking handicap. I can still bust my shit." I snapped.

"Why didn't you bust your shit when them niggas popped yo hoe ass?" Zeke asked while laughing.

As much as I didn't want to laugh, I couldn't help but snicker. He got on my fucking nerves.

"You know why I didn't shoot, Bitch! I left my shit in the whip on some dumb shit." I admitted.

"Look Bro, we know this shit is eating at you, and I promise you will get your revenge. I'll save the kill for you after we snatch these niggas up. But you can't protect anyone if you're dead. Let us do what we do best." Kenzo said sternly.

I wanted to argue and talk my shit until they agreed with me. But deep down, I knew they were right.

"Fine," I said through gritted teeth. "But I want updates. Constantly."

"You'll be the first to know." Zeke promised.

As the meeting ended, I sat back in the wheelchair angry at the world.

I didn't know who had pulled the trigger, but one thing was certain... them bitch ass niggas were going to regret ever being born.

Chapter Sixteen

Cassie

The sun had fallen, and everyone had left to go to their own homes, except for me and Carlie. Genesis offered to take her with them, but Carlie was too worried about her "Jabbie" to leave. The house was a lot quieter now and I had just finished helping Adara clean up the kitchen when I decided to check on Carlie and Jabari.

Carlie had been glued to Jabari's side since breakfast, asking him a hundred questions about his wheelchair and why he couldn't walk right now. To his credit, Jabari answered every question with patience, humor, and just enough exaggeration to keep her entertained.

When I stepped into the living room, I saw them sitting together near the big bay window. Carlie was perched on the arm of the couch, her face lit up with excitement as she showed Jabari her new American Girl Doll. He sat back, with his wheelchair pushed to the side, letting her do whatever she wanted while pretending to be annoyed. I could tell he loved the attention she was giving him.

"You better not tell no one you had me playing with dolls little girl." he said, though there was a smile tugging at the corners of his lips.

Carlie giggled. "Why not? Dolls are cool! Right, Mommy?"

I leaned against the doorway, watching them with my heart full. "That's right, baby. But Jabari's pretty cool too."

Jabari raised an eyebrow, and his sexy eyes locked with mine. "You hear that? Your mama knows what's up."

Carlie huffed dramatically. "She's just saying that because she likes you."

Heat rushed to my face, and I shot her a playful glare. "Alright, Carlie, why don't you go play for a bit?"

Carlie slid off the couch, a mischievous grin on her face.

"Okay, but I'll be back!" She skipped out of the room, leaving me alone with Jabari.

I moved to sit on the couch beside him, tucking my legs under me. Jabari tilted his head to look at me, and I shook my head at the fact that he looked so damn good even all shot the fuck up.

"She's a good kid. Smart as fuck, too. Gets that shit from her mama, I'm guessing." he said.

"Of course. What's up with you though? How are you holding up?" I teased, nudging his shoulder gently.

He shrugged, but I could see him gritting his teeth by the muscles in his jaw.

"Even better cuz you're here. The pain is a bitch, but it's manageable. This whole wheelchair thing though? Not a fan. Zero fucking stars. I do NOT recommend!" he stressed making me crack the fuck up.

"You'll be out of it soon stop bitching. You're lucky the

bullet didn't do more damage." I said, reaching over to touch his hand.

"Yeah. Lucky." he said quietly.

I watched as his eyes darkened for a moment, and then quickly went back to normal. The shit was scary and sexy at the same time.

I squeezed his hand, and his gaze flicked to mine. For a moment, neither of us said anything. It was like we both wanted to say something. Like something was waiting to be acknowledged.

"Cassie... I don't want you with anybody else." he said finally pissing me off.

"I know you not about to start this dumb shit again!" I snapped.

"Nah, nah! Wait, just listen! I mean... Shit! Look man..." he said, leaning closer.

"I don't want to see you with another nigga. As a matter of fact, I bet not ever see you with another nigga! You are mine and I'm yours. That's my pussy and this big ass dick is all yours." he added possessively.

I swallowed hard, trying to ignore the butterflies erupting in my stomach and the throbbing of my coochie.

"Oh, so you're staking a claim now?" I asked for clarification.

"Damn right I am. I mean, unless you are cool with seeing me with someone else?" he asked mischievously.

I smacked my lips, matching his energy.

"Try me if you want to mufucka!"

He nodded, as if satisfied with my answer. "Good, cuz I don't want to be with anybody else either."

I tilted my head with a grin spreading across my face. "So, we go together now?"

Jabari laughed, and the sound of his deep and rich voice made me clench my thighs.

"I guess so Mama. But…" He stopped as he glanced away for a moment before looking back at me.

"Look, I've never been in a relationship before. Honestly, I don't even believe in them shits, really. But… For you, I will try. Just don't be telling everybody and shit. I got a reputation to uphold." He joked, but his vulnerability showed through vividly.

My heart swelled at his words, and I leaned forward, resting my forehead against his. "You don't have to be perfect, Jabari. Just be real with me, and we'll figure it out."

He didn't respond right away, but his hand slid to the back of my neck, pulling me closer. Our lips met, and he immediately began sucking on my bottom lip making me moan lowly. He began kissing me like he was pouring every unspoken word into it.

When we finally broke apart, I rested my head on his shoulder, letting the moment linger.

"You know, I never thought I would see the day." I said softly.

"Yeah, but I'm glad it happened. It feels right. Plus, I knew you wanted a nigga. You were just tryna play hard to get." he replied playfully.

Before I could respond, the front door swung open.

"Damn, Jabari! You looking cozy as hell in here. Let me find out niggas ain't scared of love no more!" Zeke's voice boomed, and I jumped looking guilty as hell.

Kenzo followed, grinning like a damn fool. "That nigga wasn't fooling nobody! We knew what it was back at the club."

Jabari groaned, leaning back against the couch. "Man, can y'all mind your business?"

"Not when it's this entertaining. Cassie, welcome to the family." Zeke said, leaning against the doorframe.

I laughed nervously, hiding my face in my hands. Jabari reached over, pulling me closer to him.

"Go ahead, clown all you want. I'm still not fucked up in head like y'all niggas!" Jabari snapped making us all laugh.

Zeke and Kenzo exchanged amused looks before retreating, leaving us alone again.

Jabari glanced at me with a smirk on his handsome face. "I guess it's not a secret anymore."

"Nigga it never was!" Zeke yelled from the kitchen making me crack up laughing and Jabari smack his lips in annoyance.

As much as I hated the idea of being the center of attention, I couldn't deny how happy I felt. I was no longer single, and I had a psycho as my man who has never been in a relationship. So many things could go wrong, but shit for Jabari... I'm willing to take that risk.

CHAPTER
Seventeen

Jabari

Freedom tasted sweeter than I expected. It had been weeks since the shooting, and while I still felt a lil ache every now and then, the doctor's clearance was exactly what I needed. I'd been suffocating under everyone's watchful eyes, and as much as I loved my family, I was ready to get back to my own space.

I couldn't even get no pussy without a mufucka knocking on the door interrupting. Plus, Cassie said we couldn't fuck until the doctor cleared me. She's been sucking my dick lovely, but I need that wet shit. She doesn't have any excuses now! I was cleared and back home!

But I wasn't going alone.

Cassie and Carlie were coming with me. That shit wasn't up for debate. The second she agreed to be mine was the second we became one. We must move as a fucking unit at all times.

Cassie, of course, had been hesitant. She liked her independence, and her space. I respected that, but I also wasn't about to give her the option to say no. If there was one thing the shooting taught me, it was that life was too short to waste time. I hired a moving company and had them transport all of her shit right after the doctor said I could go home this morning.

Cassie and Carlie were mine now, and I wanted them close.

"Jabari, this is crazy," Cassie said as she stood in front of my new SUV that I bought as a *PULL GIFT*.

See, pregnant women get push gifts cuz they push a baby out their pussies. I bought myself a pull gift cuz I pulled the fuck through after getting popped. Simple math!

"What's crazy?" I asked, leaning against the vehicle with a smirk.

"This! You didn't even fucking ask me. You just… did it." she said, gesturing to the movers loading up her boxes and furniture.

"You should know by now that I never ask Mama. Plus, your place is empty now, so you might as well come home with me and Princess Carlie." I said simply.

Her lips parted like she wanted to argue, but I held up a hand.

"Before you start, there's one more thing I need to show you." I hurried out.

She narrowed her eyes curiously. "What else Jabari? Show me what?"

"You'll see. Hop in." I said, opening the passenger door for her.

The drive was quiet, except for Carlie humming along

to the radio in the back seat. When we finally pulled up to the building, Cassie frowned.

"Where are we?" she asked, stepping out of the car.

I didn't answer right away, just walked toward the glass doors of the small building. It had been cleaned up nicely, and the new sign was still waiting to be installed. However, I could already see her name on it in my head.

"Jabari?" she pressed, following me inside.

I turned to face her with my hands in my pockets. "This is yours."

She blinked, looking around the space. "What?"

"This building. I copped it for you. For the spa you've been talking about." I said.

Her hands flew to her mouth as she looked around in shock.

"You're fucking lying!" she squealed.

"Do I look like I would play about some shit like that?" I asked.

Then I pulled out a black card from my pocket and held it out to her.

"Here. Use this to furnish the place however you want. No limit. Make this mufucka yours Mama." I told her happily.

She stared at the card, then at me, then back at the card. Her hands trembled as she took it.

"Babyyyy… I can't… This is too much." She whined.

"Nah. It's not enough. You've been talking about opening your own spa since I met you. I know you were saving to do it on your own, but you will never have to do anything by yourself again. I got you and Carlie for life. Take that money that you were saving and ball out however you like. This here is on me." I said seriously.

Tears spilled down her cheeks, and she covered her face, her shoulders shaking. I stepped closer, pulling her into my arms.

"Why are you crying Mama?" I asked, pressing a kiss to her hair.

"Becauseeee! No one has ever done anything like this for me before." she cried against my chest.

"Well, get used to it. You're with me now, Cassie. I take care of what's mine." I said softly.

"Mommy this is your spa! Can you make an area for little girls?" Carlie asked excitedly making us laugh.

"That's actually a great idea Princess! I sure can!" Cassie replied happily.

Carlie squealed and danced in circles. I was just happy that they both liked the place!

By the time we made it to my place, Carlie had fallen asleep in the back seat, and Cassie had calmed down. Her cheeks were still a little pink from all the crying and her eyes were puffy. Still, she was beautiful and those were happy tears.

"Me casa es su casa!" I said as we pulled into the driveway.

Cassie looked up at the house and rolled her eyes playfully. "Boy eff you!"

I smirked. "I got you later Mama."

After carrying Carlie inside and settling her into one of the guest rooms, I gave Cassie the grand tour. The last time she was here, we were in my room, the kitchen and the living room. She never got a chance to see the entire house.

As I showed her around, she was quiet, taking everything in, and I could tell she was overwhelmed.

When we finally made it to my bedroom, I closed the door behind us and leaned against it, watching her as she wandered around the room.

"Still think moving in was a bad idea?" I asked.

She turned to face me, a small smile on her lips. "I don't know what to think, Jabari. This is all so much, so fast…"

"Then don't think. Just go with the flow and if it becomes too much, I'll build you a house in the backyard." I said, pushing off the door and walking toward her.

She giggled as I cupped her face, brushing my thumb over her cheek.

"Cassie, I've wanted this for a long time but was afraid to admit the shit. My fault for making moves without discussing them with you first, but that's going to be a hard habit to break. If this is too much for you, let me know now. I'll fall back and we can take this shit slow." I said seriously.

Her eyes searched mine, and then she shook her head. "I guess you don't have to break in my house no more."

I nodded happier than a nigga losing his virginity.

"Is it really breaking? You can't break in somewhere you have a key to." I replied shrugging.

"Nigga I never you a… you know what? Nevermind!" She said laughing.

She likes that crazy shit!

I leaned in and kissed her slowly, savoring the softness of her lips and the way her body melted against mine. Everything about the moment felt right, like this was where we were always meant to end up.

After eating dinner as a family and watching movies with Carlie until she fell asleep, we raced to our room. The second the door closed, we were on each other like flies on shit. I wasn't in her pussy two minutes before I was nutting. I had no shame in my game either. She should've never held that shit from me. I fucked her nice and long in the shower though to make up and after that, a nigga was exhausted.

When it was over, we lay tangled together with her head resting on my chest.

"You good?" I asked, running my fingers through her hair.

"Better than good," she said softly.

I smiled, pulling her closer. A nigga was spoken for and though I'm terrified, I'm also content. Cassie and Carlie were here, and they weren't going any fucking where.

Chapter Eighteen

Cassie

"Good morning, sleepyhead." Jabari's voice came from the doorway sending a shiver down my spine.

I turned to see him leaning against the frame, with a small smirk on his face and a mug of coffee in his hand. I didn't even know that nigga drank coffee. He was shirtless and had on some pajama pants that did little to hide that COCK in between his legs.

"Morning Baby. I didn't know you drank coffee." I murmured, sitting up and pulling the blankets around me.

"Shit, I didn't. Maybe I'm turning over a new leaf," he teased, walking over and handing it to me.

I raised an eyebrow, taking the mug. "Uh-huh. What do you want?"

Jabari grinned, sitting on the edge of the bed. "Can't a man just take care of his woman without an ulterior motive?"

I rolled my eyes but couldn't help the smile tugging at my lips. "If that's the case, thank you."

He leaned down, brushing his lips against mine in a soft kiss that made my toes curl. God, I adore this man!

After breakfast and a quick shower, I checked my phone to find a missed call from my mom. I called her back as I got ready for the day. Jabari had taken Carlie out for some ice cream and then to Zeke's house for a playdate with Zahra. I thought it was the cutest shit ever.

"Hey, Mommy!" I said, slipping on a pair of sandals.

"Cassie! Baby, how are you?" she asked sweetly.

"I'm good, Mommy. Just getting ready to head to the spa." I explained.

I called my mom and told her about the building Jabari got me and she was so happy she cried. She had met Jabari a few weeks ago and fell in love with his ole charming ass. She told me that she felt he was more my speed than Sam was and that tickled me.

"That's wonderful, sweetheart. I've been telling everyone about how you're about to open your own place. Your cousins were asking about you the other day." she said.

I froze mid-step. "My cousins?"

"Yes, Tina, Shya, and Cresha. They asked how you were doing and said they'd love to reconnect and catch up." she said.

I nearly laughed out loud. Those three hadn't cared about me since I was old enough to tie my own shoes.

"Reconnect huh?" I asked skeptically.

"They've grown up, Cassie. Maybe it's time to let

bygones be bygones." Mom said with a hint of reproach in her voice.

I sighed, sitting down on the edge of the bed. "I don't know, Mom. They made my life miserable growing up. Always calling me stuck-up, saying I thought I was better than them. And for what? Because I didn't act ghetto and stupid like them?"

"They were jealous. You always had your head on straight. That's still not a reason to hold onto grudges forever." she said softly.

Her words sat heavy on my chest. "I'll think about it," I said, not ready to commit to anything.

———

Later that morning, I met Genesis at the spa. She was already there when I arrived, standing in the middle of the main room with a clipboard in hand.

"This place is perfect. My brother did his big one!" she said as I walked in.

I nodded, smiling as I looked around the space. It still needed a lot of work, but I could already see my vision coming to life.

"He did," I said softly.

Genesis glanced at me, raising an eyebrow. "What's wrong? You look like you've got something on your mind."

I hesitated, then told her about my mom's call and the conversation about my cousins.

"Do you think I should call them?" I asked.

Genesis shrugged, leaning against the counter. "Depends. Do you want to reconnect with them?"

"I don't know. A part of me feels like it's not worth the drama, but another part of me wonders if things could be different now that we're older." I admitted.

She nodded thoughtfully. "People change, Cassie. But don't get your hopes up too high. If they're still the same, you'll only end up disappointed. Approach it with caution. And let them hoes know that you aren't a child anymore and we ain't fighting. We shooting bitches."

Her advice made sense, and I decided to take the plunge. After we finished going over plans for the spa, I called my mom and asked for one of their numbers. What's the worst that could happen? Besides, as my girl said, we shooting bitches! They better tread lightly!

That evening, after tucking Carlie into bed, I sat on the couch with my phone in hand, staring at the number. My heart raced as I debated whether or not to press call.

"Just do it," I whispered to myself, hitting the button before I could chicken out.

The phone rang twice before a voice answered.

"Hello?"

"Tina?" I asked nervously.

"Yeah, who's this?"

"It's Cassie."

There was a pause, and for a moment, I thought she might hang up.

"Well, well. Long time, no talk." she said finally.

"Yeah. My mama said y'all asked about me." I said awkwardly.

"Something like that. How you been though?" she said, her tone guarded.

I told her a little about my life, keeping it vague, and she shared bits and pieces about hers. To my surprise, the conversation was pleasant. We even laughed a couple of times.

By the time we hung up, we'd made plans to meet in a couple of days. I decided not to bring Carlie, just in case things went sideways, but who knows. If things go smoothly, I'll open up more. Baby steps though!

The next morning, I woke up to the sound of laughter coming from downstairs. Curious, I got out of bed and followed the noise to the living room, where I found Jabari and Carlie playing a game.

"Gotcha!" Carlie squealed as she tagged Jabari, who pretended to fall over dramatically.

"You got me!" he groaned, clutching his chest.

I leaned against the doorway, smiling as I watched them. Seeing them together like this made my heart swell.

"Good morning!" I sang, stepping into the room.

"Mommy!" Carlie ran over to me, wrapping her arms around my legs.

"Morning, Mama. You sleep okay? You were knocked out when we got in last night." Jabari said, sitting up and grinning at me.

"I slept great actually. What are you two up to?" I said, ruffling Carlie's hair.

"Just having some fun. You've got a busy day ahead, right?" he said, standing up and stretching.

I nodded. "Yeah, but this was a nice way to start it."

He walked over and kissed my forehead. "Go get ready. We'll be here when you get back."

As I drove to the spa later that day, I couldn't help but reflect on how much my life had changed in such a short time. Jabari and Carlie had brought so much light into my world, and now I had a chance to mend old wounds with my family.

Let me find out Jabari had been the missing puzzle piece all along!

CHAPTER Nineteen

Jabari

I woke up this morning with one thing on my mind. Murder. My patience was gone, and I wanted some fucking answers or bodies are about to start dropping. It had been weeks since I got shot, and we still didn't know who did it. That shit has me hotter than fish grease!

Kenzo leaned back on the leather couch, his arms stretched out like he didn't have a care in the world. His too school for cool ass gets on my damn nerves sometimes. If I wasn't sure he would beat my ass, I would bust him in his shit. I'm a crazy mufucka, but that shit is suicide.

"You pacing isn't gonna make answers appear, Jabari." Kenzo barked.

I shot him a glare, but he only smirked.

"And you sitting there like King Tut isn't helping either muthafucka." I spat.

Xander chuckled from his spot near the window, in amusement. "He's got a point, Kenzo. Maybe you should get up and do a little pacing too."

Kenzo flipped him off without moving from his spot, and the room filled with laughter. Normally, I'd be the first to jump in with a sarcastic remark, but my mood was too sour.

Adonis set down his glass of whiskey and crossed his arms. "We'll find out who it was, Jabari. These things take time. We don't want to move sloppy and all of us get cuffed up."

"I don't have time. What if they come back and try to catch me slipping again? Only this time, I have Cassie or Carlie with me!" I snapped, running a hand over my face.

Zeke, who had been quietly scrolling through something on his phone, looked up. "We've got your back. You know that. Whoever did this is going to regret it. But you walking around here all wound up isn't going to fix anything."

I knew they were right, but that shit didn't make me feel any better.

The conversation shifted when Xander, never one to miss an opportunity to piss me off, raised an eyebrow at me. "Speaking of family... How's Cassie?"

The mention of her name made my dick stiffen.

"She's good Nigga." I said, trying to keep my tone neutral.

Kenzo grinned. "Good, huh? That's all you've got? Come on, man, we're your brothers. Spill."

I rolled my eyes.

"Ain't shit to spill nosey ass niggas!" I snapped.

"Oh, there's plenty hoe ass nigga! Let's not forget you

are the same nigga who swore up and down that love was for pussies. What was that bullshit you used to say? 'Relationships are for bitches. I got enough dick for all my hoes.'" Adonis said, smirking.

Zeke laughed, his deep voice filling the room. "And don't forget when he used to clown us for settling down. Called us all kinds of whipped pussies."

"Because y'all were! I mean, come on Zeke. You turned soft when you were still a damn kid. You didn't even count. But you other niggas... Y'all went from running the streets to playing house. That shit was lame as hell, but funny to watch." I said, throwing my hands up.

"Funny, huh? What's funny now is how you're all up Cassie's ass. Don't think we don't notice how you light up like a virgin when her name gets brought up." Xander said, leaning forward with a wicked grin.

Kenzo nodded. "Yeah, nigga. You're whipped just like us. Just admit the shit."

I sighed, shaking my head. "Alright, man damn. I care about her. A lot."

The room went quiet for a second. I'm guessing everyone was shocked that I admitted it out loud.

"She's different. She doesn't just let me get away with my usual bullshit. She calls me out, makes me want to do better. Not just for her, but for Carlie too. She deserves my all, and I'm trying to figure out how to give it to her without changing myself too much." I continued.

Adonis gave me a long look before speaking. "That's real. You don't have to change yourself, just don't half ass it, Jabari. If you're in, be all in. You know Cassie's been through enough."

"I know," I said, nodding. "Her past with Carlie's

Pops...it's like she's been waiting for someone to show her what love's supposed to look like. I want to be that for her. But shit, outside of my family, I don't know what the shit looks like my damn self. I'm going to give the shit my all though."

Kenzo clapped me on the shoulder. "Then stop worrying about what you used to say and just do it. You've got this. If we could do this shit, then I know you could!"

He said making us all laugh. We used to run through these hoes! Man, those were the days!

By the time I got home, my mood had settled some. Walking through the door and seeing Cassie sitting on the couch with her laptop open in front of her and Carlie coloring at the coffee table, felt like coming up for air after being underwater.

"You're back!" Cassie said, glancing up and smiling.

"Yeah. Y'all miss me?" I said, dropping my keys on the counter.

Carlie looked up and grinned. "Nope!"

Cassie laughed. "Don't let her fool you. She kept asking when you'd be home."

"Snitch!" Carlie said, giggling.

I walked over and ruffled her hair. "Good to know I was missed, even if you won't admit it."

Cassie closed her laptop and stretched. "How was your day?"

I sat down beside her, pulling her feet into my lap. "It was alright. Them niggas were on my case, though. They wouldn't let me forget how much shit I used to talk shit about relationships and shit."

Cassie smirked. "Hmm, what shit did you used to say?"

I laughed, shaking my head. "Nothing important woman. But enough about me. How was your day?"

Cassie's expression softened. "Everything was smooth. I found a vendor to make my smocks and banners for the Spa. Oh, and I talked to my mom. She's been on me about reconnecting with my cousins."

"Your cousins?" I asked, raising an eyebrow.

"Yeah," she said, growing serious.

"Tina, Cresha, and Shya. We had a... strained relationship growing up. They used to bully me, steal my toys and clothes, and just make my life hell. I started standing up for myself as I got older, but by then, the damage was done. I distanced myself from them completely." She continued.

"Sounds like they were jealous, as fuck." I said.

"They were. But my mom thinks it's time to let all that go and try to rebuild something." she admitted.

I didn't even hesitate. "I'll go with you."

Cassie looked at me, surprised. "You don't have to do that."

"I know, but I want to. I wish them hoes would try to bully you now. I'll shoot a hoe in the coochie for you!" I said and I was dead ass serious.

Her eyes softened, and she reached out to touch my face. "Thank you, Baby."

"You can thank me when Princess Carlie goes to sleep." I said mischievously, leaning in to kiss her.

That night, as I lay in bed with Cassie curled up beside me, and Carlie sound asleep in her bedroom that she said she liked more than her old bedroom, I felt content. I gave her complete freedom on how she wanted to decorate it. And if course the entire room is Princess themed.

I stared down at Cassie's face as she snored lightly against my chest and smirked. This love shit is kinda cool. I fuck with it.

Chapter Twenty

Cassie

The car ride to my aunt's house felt like it lasted forever, even though it was only a fifteen-minute drive. My mom suggested sitting in the backseat, while I sat up front looking out the window while Jabari drove. I loved how he knew I was antsy, so he kept his hand resting casually on my knee.

"You okay?" he asked, glancing at me.

I nodded, though my stomach was doing somersaults.

"Yeah, just nervous. It's been years since I've seen them, and things weren't exactly...great back then."

My mom tapped my shoulder, and I turned around to see what she wanted.

"That's why we're doing this, Cassie. Time heals all wounds. You're older now, and so are they. Things will be different. And if not, at least you can say you tried!" She offered.

I wanted to believe her, but the pit in my stomach said otherwise. I pray I don't fuck no one up today.

Jabari squeezed my knee. "Don't worry about it. If they start acting up, we gone light their asses up."

That simple statement sent a wave of calm through me. Jabari always had my back, and knowing he'd be there made me feel like I could handle anything. I loved that crazy shit, I swear.

When we pulled up to the house, I took a deep breath. My mom smiled at me encouragingly, and Jabari leaned over to kiss my forehead. "You've got this, baby."

The house smelled like a mix of baked ham and sweet potatoes, a nostalgic scent that reminded me of family gatherings when I was little. My aunt welcomed us with open arms, and for a moment, I felt like this might actually go smoothly.

Tina, Cresha, and Shya were already seated at the dining table. Shya's face lit up when she saw me.

"Cassie! It's been so long!" she exclaimed, jumping up to hug me.

"It really has. You look great." I said, hugging her back.

And I wasn't lying. Her shape was sick, and her makeup was on point!

She laughed. "Thanks, girl. So do you. That dress is fire."

The warmth of her welcome eased some of my nerves, but the icy glances from Tina and Cresha reminded me that not everyone was happy to see me. Which had me ready to snap already cuz bitch y'all wanted me here! The fuck!

"Cassie. Look at you. All grown up and fancy." Tina said, her voice dripping with fake sweetness.

I smiled tightly. "Good to see you, Tina."

"Yeah, it's been a while. Guess you've been too busy to visit the family." Cresha added, her tone was just as condescending.

Jabari's hand on my lower back reminded me that I didn't have to turn up like I normally would. My man is here, and he is shooting bitches over me! I plastered on another smile and simply said, "Life's been busy, but I'm glad we're here now."

"And who is this that you have with you?" Tina asked while nodding toward Jabari.

"This is my man Jabari." I replied shortly.

"Hmmm, okay!" She said before switching off.

Weak ass hoes!

As the afternoon went on, I tried to focus on reconnecting with Shya. We laughed about old times, shared updates on our lives, and for a moment, it felt like the years of distance hadn't existed.

"I heard you're opening a spa! That's so dope Cuz!" Shya said, her eyes bright with excitement.

"Yeah, I am. It's been a dream of mine for years, and I'm finally making it happen." I said, smiling.

"Yes, I'm so proud of my baby!" My mom said happily.

Before I could say more, Tina chimed in. "A spa, huh? That's...interesting. Guess you're trying to make up for all that time you spent doing nothing."

My smile faltered, but I kept my cool. I could smell a

jealous hoe from miles away. I guess some things never change. "I've worked hard to get here. It hasn't been easy, but my life is amazing actually."

Cresha leaned back in her chair, smirking. "Well, let's hope it lasts. Businesses like that don't always stick around, you know. It's so much competition in the Spa business."

I caught the shady emphasis she put in "Spa" too. These hoes... Whew!

Jabari leaned down and whispered in my ear, "You better say something, or I will. The fuck is up with these bitches!"

I shook my head slightly. "I got this baby. As soon as shit goes left, I'll handle it." I whispered back.

He didn't look convinced, but he nodded.

And boy did shit go left! When Jabari excused himself to go to the restroom. I noticed Tina slip away shortly after, but I was too busy trying to keep the conversation with Shya going to think much of it. Plus, I trusted my man. The nigga is crazy, but he ain't that crazy.

When Jabari returned, his entire demeanor had changed. His jaw was tight, and his eyes were colder than I'd ever seen them.

"What's wrong?" I asked angrily.

He was fine before he left...

"Nothing." he said, sitting down beside me.

"Jabari now is not the time to start lying in this relationship. What the fuck happened?" I said, narrowing my eyes.

He shook his head. "We'll talk about it later."

"No. We'll talk about it now. If you don't tell me, I swear I'll knock all this shit over and make a fucking scene." I said firmly.

He sighed, running a hand over his face. "Aight, chill."

Lowering his voice, he leaned closer to me. "Tina stopped me outside the bathroom. At first, she was on some weird shit trying to reach for my dick..."

I shot up from my seat ready to go and break that hoe's nose! Unfortunately, he grabbed me and stopped me.

"Aye! Chill man! I handled the shit!" He barked lowly.

"Handled it how? Not good enough apparently cuz the bitch is still breathing!" I snapped.

"This is exactly why I wanted to wait and tell you. Now are you going to let me finish or what?" he asked annoyedly.

I rolled my eyes and nodded for him to continue.

"After I threatened to shoot her in the titty, she said some shit about me needing to watch my back because you're 'known for setting niggas up.' Then she hinted that you had something to do with Carlie's pop's death." He concluded.

My heart stopped. I don't think I had ever been so fucking mad in my life. "She said what?"

Jabari nodded.

"And you believed her... That's why you came in here all mad and shit." I assumed.

He ran his hand down his face with a deep sigh. "Look, I won't lie and say it didn't pique my interest."

I shook my head in disbelief and had to laugh to stop myself from crying. I could feel my mom's eyes on us trying to figure out what was going on.

"Hear me out man! I just got robbed so you know my trust is fucked up. And you know the bullshit Genesis and her hoe ass brother was into. But I swear to God on my OG's I didn't believe her. I know you wouldn't do no shit like that. I was mad because I don't know who else she is feeding this bullshit to. I'm worried about a mufucka trying to come after you on some revenge shit." He explained.

I exhaled a breath that I didn't know I was holding. I was happy that he believed I wouldn't do no shit like that, but it did make me nervous about his concerns. Was this bitch out here spreading lies about me? Are mufuckas out here thinking I'm setting niggas up? Oh hell naw!

I stood up, my chair scraping loudly against the floor. "Excuse me for a moment." I said sternly.

"Baby, do you want me to shoot the bitch?" Jabari asked, grabbing my hand.

I shook him off, my blood boiling. "Nah, this bitch is lightwork. Always has been. That's why she always needed her sisters to back her up. Just make sure these hoes don't jump me." I joked but was halfway serious.

"I wish a muthafucka would! I heard everything. I'm sorry I even asked you to reach out to that little bitch! Whoop her ass and let's get the hell out of here!" My mom spat angrily making Jabari laugh.

Oh, it's really up now!

I found Tina in the kitchen, chatting with Cresha like she hadn't just tried to ruin my entire relationship and reputation.

"Tina." I said.

She turned, feigning innocence. "What, Cassie?"

"You wanna do this in here or do you want go outside?" I asked, crossing my arms.

Cresha snickered. "Oh, here we go."

Tina rolled her eyes.

"Girl..."

I didn't even let her finish that sentence. I swung and bust her right in her nose.

"Oh shit!" I heard Jabari shout.

I didn't stop there. As soon as her weak ass dropped, I was on her as like white on rice! I stood over her and started pounding her shit!

"You wanted a reaction out of me, well here you go bitch!" I screamed.

"Oh my God! Cassie stop! Someone grab her!" I heard my aunt yell.

"Nope! Your daughter has mine fucked up! She needed this ass whooping a long time ago!" My mom shouted.

"Ah ah ah! I wouldn't do that if I were you! You touch my girl, I'm gone forget you have a coochie and beat yo ass!" Jabari said and it took everything in me not to laugh.

"Get this bitch off me!" Tina screamed.

By now, I was sitting on her chest delivering nothing but face shots! This bitch was gonna remember this ass whooping for a long time.

"This is fucked up! Shya! Do something bitch! Why are you just standing there?!" Cresha shouted.

"I told y'all not to start no drama. Y'all are still messy, and I don't have shit to do with that! She shouldn't start shit if she can't fucking fight!" Shya said calmly.

"Alright baby. That's enough. Jabari grab her before she kills the damn girl." My mom yelled.

He lifted me by the waist and kissed the side of my neck.

"Calm down tiger!" He sang in my ear.

"I'm cool. I'm good!" I said out of breath.

He reluctantly released me and as soon as I was back on the floor, I kicked that bitch in her face.

"Oh shit! Cassie!" Jabari yelled through laughter.

His crazy ass would find the shit funny.

"That was for tryna grab my man's dick bitch!" I snapped.

My aunt stepped in front of me trying to block my view of Tina with her hands raised in the air. "I didn't bring everyone together for this nonsense. I can't believe you Cassie! You need to leave."

"Well, I've been kicked out of better places!" Jabari huffed before storming out with me and my mom laughing behind him.

On the way out, I exchanged glances with Shya. She smirked at me, and I nodded my head smirking back. Despite the shitty way the night ended, I actually enjoyed catching up with her. I will definitely keep in touch with her.

———

The car ride home was silent as everyone's adrenaline came down. Jabari reached over and took my hand, his thumb brushing over my knuckles.

"You okay?" he asked softly.

"No. But I will be." I admitted.

We dropped my mom off who kept apologizing every three seconds. I told her that it was not her fault, and I was being honest. She didn't raise them messy hoes. When we got home, I sat on the couch, trying to process everything. Jabari sat beside me, pulling me into his arms.

"Don't let them get to you. Them hoes are just jealous. You've done something with your life, and they hate that shit." he said.

I nodded, resting my head against his chest. "Thank you for not believing that shit she said. I would never set you up, let alone do anything to hurt you."

He kissed the top of my head. "You don't have to convince me Mama. I know what we have. And if bitches are mad now, just wait until we really turn up on they ass."

I looked up at him and smiled.

"Come on. I need a massage. I'm sore as fuck." I cried out making him laugh.

"Old ass out here fighting like you young and shit! Bring yo ass on." He replied while standing up.

I giggled like a little girl as he lifted me from the couch.

"Just know this massage will include a happy ending!" He added.

I laughed as he ran to the bedroom with me in his arms.

CHAPTER Twenty-One

Jabari

Here I was up again and unable to sleep. Cassie was curled up beside me, snoring like she was getting some of the best sleep she ever had. But again... I couldn't sleep. Every time I closed my eyes, I'd see flashes of the night I got shot. Remembering the pain vividly.

I shifted slightly, trying not to wake her, but my hand instinctively went to her hip, pulling her closer. My mind was everywhere, but I knew I needed her near me. Cassie was my peace. She brought out another side of me that I didn't know existed. She made me calm.

But even as I let myself enjoy the feeling of her, something nagged at me. The shit was like an itch in the back of my mind that I couldn't scratch to save my life. The comment Tina made at dinner kept playing over and over in my head: *"You better watch your back."*

I'd shrugged the shit off at the moment, but I couldn't shake the feeling that there was more to it. So, I had Zeke do some digging for me.

I decided to try and push my thoughts to the said and wake Cassie up in the best way possible... with this dick inside of her. As soon as I was about to lift her leg and dive in, my phone buzzed loudly on the nightstand, pissing me the fuck off.

I groaned, reaching for it. Whoever it was better have a damn good reason for calling me while I was about to go deep sea diving.

"Yeah?" I muttered, keeping my voice low so I didn't wake Cassie.

"Nigga you were right! That mufucka set the whole robber and shooting up!" Zeke said loudly.

I sat up immediately. "Talk to me. Tell me something good!"

"Sam set that whole thing up!" Zeke said bluntly.

I frowned. I had suspicions that he would be mad, but I didn't think he would be the one to actually put some shit together like that. "Sam and who?"

"He set you up, Bro. It wasn't random. His cousins were the ones who pulled the trigger, but he was behind the whole thing. He told them that you had a lot of money and drugs." Zeke explained.

The words hit me like a sledgehammer. I swung my legs out of bed and smiled in disbelief. Punk ass Sam had some balls after all.

"How did you find out?" I asked.

"Nigga do you know who I am? I find everything out! Besides, Sam's been running his mouth like a little bitch to the wrong people. He didn't think you'd survive, but now that you have, he's laying low. We've got his location. He's hiding out at his cousin's place just outside of town." Zeke replied.

"Send me the address." I said eagerly.

"Already did. I'm heading there now with Kenzo, Adonis and Xander. We'll meet you there." Zeke replied.

I hung up without another word and stood, pulling on a pair of sweatpants and a hoodie.

———

As I grabbed my gun from the drawer, I heard Cassie stir behind me.

"Baby? What's going on? Where are you going?" she murmured.

I could hear the fatigue and concern in her voice.

I turned to face her, and smirked at the sight of her sitting up, her hair tousled, her eyes half-closed. She was worried about a nigga, but she had no reason to be.

"There's something I need to take care of. Zeke called. They found out who shot me." I explained.

Her eyes widened, and she was fully awake now. "Who?"

I hesitated, but there was no point in sugarcoating the shit. "Sam."

Cassie's mouth dropped to her chest in shock. "Sam? My Sam?" She asked and I had to side eye her ass.

"My Sam?" I mimicked her.

"Nah! Your ex, you funky breath heffa!" I corrected her ass.

She rolled her eyes and then motioned with her hands for me to continue.

"Yeah, it was his ass. He set me up. One of his cousins pulled the trigger, but it was his plan. He wanted my ass dead." I explained.

Her hand flew to her mouth as she gasped. "Oh my God."

I stepped closer and grabbed her hands. "I need to go handle this, but I will be back."

Cassie shook her head, her eyes filling with tears. "I can't tell you not to go because I would be wasting my breath, but please be careful and come back to me.

"I promise I will be back before you know it. I just have to see this through. His hoe ass tried to kill me, Mama. He wanted me out of the way, and I'm going to show him just how bad of an idea that shit was." I said firmly.

She looked torn. "Let me come with you."

"No. Hell no." I said immediately.

"You're staying here. I need to know you and Carlie are safe. I can't focus if I'm worrying about you." I said seriously.

"But—"

"No," I repeated, cupping her face in my hands. "Cassie, listen to me. I'll be okay. I'll come back to you. I promise."

She looked at me as tears spilled down her cheeks.

"I hate this." she whined.

"I know, but I have to go." I said softly.

Finally, she nodded, though I could see how much it fucked with her.

"Be careful, Jabari. Please." She begged.

I kissed her on the forehead and then on the lips. "I will."

I was almost out the door when I heard her call my name.

"What up Mama?" I asked.

"Make his ass suffer." She spat.

I nodded evilly. "Come on Mama. You already know how I'm coming."

By the time I pulled up to the location Zeke had sent, my brothers were already there, waiting outside in the cut.

"Glad you could finally join us." Xander said sarcastically.

"Let's get this shit over with." I said with my jaw clenched.

Kenzo handed me a gun, though I already had one. "You good?"

"Nigga I'm great!" I said, checking the weapon.

We moved silently, as we crept along the side of the old house where Sam was hiding. The windows were dark, but the lights inside of the house slightly showed through them.

Xander signaled for us to split up, and we surrounded the house, each of us taking a different entry point. My heart was pounding in anticipation. I couldn't wait to get my hand on these mufuckas.

This wasn't just about revenge. It was about sending a message. One that Sam and any other nigga who thought about trying me would never forget.

At Kenzo's signal, we breached the house simultaneously and forcefully. Sam's cousins were the first to react, scrambling to grab weapons, but they were too slow. Zeke took one down with a single shot to the shoulder, and Kenzo disarmed another with a swift blow to the head.

I found Sam cowering in a corner of the living room like the little bitch he was. Nigga was shaking like a tambourine on Sunday.

"Jabari! Wait, let me explain!" he stammered, holding up his hands.

"Explain what bitch? How you tried to have me killed? All because you couldn't take your L and keep it pushing!" I shouted coldly while raising my gun.

He shook his head frantically. "It wasn't personal! I just...I just wanted you out of the way so I could get Cassie back. You ruined everything!"

My blood boiled at his words. "You put a hit on me because I took your bitch? You really tried to take a nigga out?"

"It wasn't supposed to go like this! They... they were supposed to scare you, not kill you." he cried.

"Stop lying bitch! You wanted my ass gone! Stand on that shit! I already know the truth mufucka!" I said furiously.

Sam's mouth opened and closed, but no words came out.

I stepped closer, pressing the barrel of my gun to his forehead. "It's cool. Don't even matter anyways. Just know that you fucked up and now you're going to wish you never did."

———

We took Sam and his cousins back to the warehouse and tortured their asses for hours. As much as I wanted to prolong the shit, I was ready to take my ass back home and fuck my woman. A nigga tried to take me out over a woman that was never really his to begin with. What better way to celebrate their loss then by going to fuck the wig off that same woman?!

After removing limbs and burning the fuck out of them, I ended the fun by just shooting them all in the head. The message was clear: fuck with me or my family, and you die. Simple. I made sure his bitch ass looked me right in the eyes too. I hope he rots and only thinks of my handsome ass.

As I drove back home, my adrenaline was still pumping through my veins. All I could think about was Cassie. She was my anchor and kept my head straight in moments like this. I couldn't wait to get home. I was going to make sure I tattoo my name on that pussy. Nothing makes my dick harder than killing a pussy ass nigga!

CHAPTER Twenty-Two

Cassie

The door had barely closed behind Jabari when my chest tightened, and my anxiety punched the shit out of me. He hadn't been gone for more than a few minutes, but it already felt like hours. My mind was racing and jumping to the worst conclusions. No matter how much I tried to think positively, I kept reverting to the negative thoughts.

I paced the living room, with my arms wrapped tightly around myself. Carlie was fast asleep in her room, which I was very happy about. I tried turning on the TV to distract my thoughts but that shit only annoyed me. This shit was pure torture.

What if he didn't come back?

I shook the thought away and grabbed my phone. My hands trembled as I scrolled through my contacts. I hesitated for a moment before hitting Genesis' name. It was late, but shit, I didn't know who else to call.

The phone rang twice before she picked it up.

"Hey, Cassie. What are you doing up?" Genesis greeted groggily.

"Not really. Jabari just left. He—he's... Sam is the reason he got shot. He's going after Sam, and I'm... FUCK! I'm losing my mind over here." I admitted painfully.

There was a pause, and then I heard her clear her throat. "I know how you're feeling. Trust me. Kenzo has had his fair share of nights like this. He's actually gone too which leads me to believe that he's with Jabari now. Do you want me to stay on the phone with you?"

"Yes, please." I said, exhaling shakily.

"Hang tight. Let me call Pilar and the others. We've all gone through this. There is no need for you to go through this alone." she said.

Minutes later, my phone buzzed with a FaceTime request. I answered, and suddenly Genesis' face filled the screen, along with Pilar, Phoenix, and Rayne.

"Cassie. Hey Sis! First of all, I want you to breathe. You're with family now, and we've all been where you are." Pilar said, her voice gave me so much reassurance.

Rayne nodded her head as she adjusted the camera. "I had to sit through so many nights wondering if Zeke was going to come home or if I'd end up planning a funeral. It's hard, but you'll get through it. Our men are a different breed."

"And Jabari's strong. He's smart as fuck too. He won't take unnecessary risks. He's gonna fuck some shit up cuz his ass is a lil touched! But he will come back to you. They always do." Phoenix chimed in.

Their words should have been comforting, but my chest still felt tight. "I don't know how you all do this. Just sitting here, waiting...it's pure torture."

Genesis leaned closer to her screen before smiling at me. "Because we don't have a choice. We love them, and this life comes with risks. But we also know they're doing what they believe they need to do to protect us. Who are we to argue with that?"

Pilar nodded. "And we have each other. Nights like this, we're only a call away. You're one of us now, Cassie. Don't ever hesitate to call."

"Family... Guysssss!" I whined, making them laugh.

Phoenix smiled. "Yes family! And that means that you don't have to go through anything alone ever again. So, we'll stay on this call with you until Jabari walks through that door, okay?"

———

Hours passed, but I was more relaxed than I was before. My girls kept me distracted with stories, laughter, and even a few embarrassing tales about their men. Genesis talked about how Kenzo had once accidentally sent flowers to the wrong address, and she ended up beating a woman up for nothing. Phoenix shared a story about Xander trying to braid Lorenzo's hair and failing miserably.

By the time the first rays of dawn broke through the windows, I felt way better than I did before. I honestly hadn't even known that much time had passed by. I was now laying on the couch in the living room, listening to the sounds of my girls sleep. The fact that they never hung up will forever sit with me. I truly love them.

Then, finally, the sound of the front door opening made me freeze in place.

"Mama? What you still doing up?" Jabari's deep voice called out.

I quickly hung up the phone, dropped it onto the couch and ran toward him. The sight of him standing there, safe and whole, made my knees buckle. I don't think I had ever been so happy.

He caught me in his arms, holding me tightly as I clung to him like a scared child.

"I told you I would be back." he murmured against my hair.

The tears I'd been holding back all night finally spilled over. "I was so scared, Baby."

He pulled back just enough to cup my face, forcing me to look into his brown eyes. "You don't have to be scared anymore. It's over."

I exhaled shakily, breathing into his neck. "Thank God."

"And now, I need something that I can take my frustrations out on. You got something in mind?" he said with a sly smirk on his face.

I shook my head laughing. Only he would think about sex at a time like this.

"Well, what are you waiting for?"

———

After a few hours of rest, Jabari woke us up and said that he wanted us to spend the entire day together.

We spent the morning strolling through the grocery store to get the items we needed for our meals of the day. He bought me flowers. Sunflowers actually. They are my favorite. He even managed to make Carlie laugh when we stopped by a toy booth and let her pick out whatever she wanted.

By the time we got back home, I was all smiles and happier than I had ever felt. I loved spending time with my little family.

As Carlie played in the living room with her new toys, Jabari and I sat on the back porch, watching the sun set. I had a glass of wine in my hand, and he had a fat professionally rolled blunt in his.

"I need to ask you something," I said, breaking the comfortable silence.

"What's up Mama?" he said while sensually rubbing my ass.

"This life you're in," I began carefully. "The danger, the risks...how am I supposed to handle that? How am I supposed to raise my daughter in the middle of all this?"

Jabari was quiet for a moment, as he stared at the horizon.

"I won't lie to you, Cassie. It's not easy. And I won't make promises I can't keep. But I will promise you this... I'll do everything in my power to keep you and Carlie safe. You'll never have to worry about anything as long as I'm breathing. And I promise that no matter what bullshit I'm dealing with, it will never come home with me." He replied.

I swallowed hard at his response. His words were comforting and terrifying at the same damn time.

"This life isn't permanent Mama. And I promise, it if ever begins to be too much for you, I will throw in the towel." He said.

The vulnerability in his voice made my heart ache and my pussy throb. "You'd really give this up for me?"

"For you and Carlie, I would do anything." he said, leaning in to kiss me softly.

"Whew... boy I'm going to suck the skin off your dick tonight! But first, I have one other question for you." I said.

"Mannn you can't tell me no shit like that and then expect me to still want to play 21 questions!" He snapped, making me laugh.

"Relax! I just want to know besides the few times I know about, how many other times have you broken into my house?" I asked with a brow raised.

He looked away and licked his thick lips smirking.

"Only the times you knew about." He finally replied.

I side eyed him. I didn't believe that shit for one second.

"Aye man, fuck all that! I'm taking you on a real date. No interruptions, no drama. Just you and me." He said happily.

"Awwww! Our first date!" I cooed before cupping his face and giving him a kiss.

I pulled back and looked into his eyes before saying, "I love you, Jabari."

He smiled widely and if I didn't know any better, I would say his ass was blushing.

"I love you too, Mama." he said smoothly.

God! What did I do to deserve this man!!

CHAPTER Twenty-three

JABARI

I wasn't usually a nervous kinda nigga, but I guess every dog has its day. My fucking palms were sweaty, and I felt like I had to take a shit! That is rare for a nigga like me. I been in shootouts, been shot, killed niggas, and tortured mufuckas without breaking a sweat. But planning this date with Cassie had me second-guessing every move.

I glanced at my watch, making sure everything was on track. The chef was already prepping the meal, the candles were perfectly arranged, and the view from the rooftop couldn't be better. I wanted tonight to be perfect for her... no interruptions, no chaos, just us. She deserved it.

When she stepped out of the house, I had to adjust my dick in my slacks. Cassie had on this fitted black dress that hugged her curves just right, and her curls bounced as she walked toward me with a smile that made me want to say fuck this date.

"You clean up nice, Mr. Creed." she teased as she took in my suit.

"And you look exactly like you taste... fucking delicious." I said, holding out my hand to help her into the car.

Her cheeks flushed, and I couldn't help but grin as I slid into the driver's seat and pulled off.

I drove us to the rooftop of one of the tallest buildings in the city. The place was quiet and private, with a dope ass view of the skyline. I'd arranged for a private chef to prepare dinner, and soft string lights lit up the setup. The shit looked exactly like the pic I had sent Genesis. I found the idea on Pinterest. Yeah... niggas be on Pinterest too.

Cassie's eyes widened as she stepped out of the elevator and took in the scene. "Babyyyy...this is beautiful!"

I slipped my hand around her waist, guiding her to the table. "You're beautiful, Cassie. This shit is just a close second."

Dinner was perfect. We laughed, we talked and discussed plans for our future together. She told me about her dreams about the spa and everything she wants to accomplish with it. She also disclosed her plans to make it a space where women like her could feel empowered and taken care of properly.

I told her about my own dreams. About how I wanted to find a way out of the life I'd been living. How I felt like I owed this life to my father but no longer saw things that way. How I wanted to be a better man. For her. For Carlie. For us.

"I never thought I'd hear you talk like this. When I met

you, you were an asshole!" she said as she sipped her wine.

I chuckled, shaking my head. "Me either. But you changed everything for me, Cassie. You and Carlie...you make me want to be better."

Her eyes shimmered as she reached across the table to take my hand. "You are perfect."

———

After dinner, we stood at the edge of the rooftop, watching the movement below us. I wrapped my arms around her from behind, resting my chin on her shoulder.

"Thank you," she whispered, leaning back against me.

"For what?"

"For this. For showing me that there's still good in the world. And for letting me in." She replied lovingly.

I turned her around to face me and lifted her chin to look me in my eyes. Even in heels, her tiny ass only came to my chest.

"You just don't know what you mean to me."

———

Back at the house, no words were spoken when we walked through the threshold. We immediately began stripping out of our clothes and attacking each other. As soon as we were both naked, I lifted her in the air and sat her right on my dick.

"Gooodddd!" She cried out.

"That's not God Mama. This dick right here is all me!" I groaned against her lips.

I began bouncing her up and down on my dick and I could feel her juices sliding down my balls onto my thighs. Her pussy was choking my dick so tightly that my knees were buckling.

"Don't... don't you fucking drop me Jabari!" She moaned.

Not wanting to chance it, I sat down on the couch and sat back so she could do her thing. She smirked at me as she placed both feet on my sides. Then she grabbed onto my shoulders and pulled out her best Megan The Stallion moves.

"Goddamn girl! The fuck you tryna do!" I groaned.

She started slamming down harder and I had to close my eyes and pray that she got her shit off before me.

"Cassie. Baby! Shit!" I moaned.

Not wanting to go out like that, I reached under her thighs and started fucking her from under her.

"Oooh shit! Wait!" She cried.

"Nah! Ain't no wait! Let me feel that shit! Wet my shit up Mama!" I coached her.

"Fuck! Here it comes!" She screamed.

I was happy Carlie was gone with her mom because baby girl would be traumatized.

"I'm finna nut Mama! Shit!" I moaned.

"Me tooooo!" She screamed.

We came together and I caught a fucking cramp in my leg. Pain and all that shit was magnificent.

I woke up the next morning with Cassie curled up against me. Her hair was sprawled across the pillow, and we were lying on top of the covers. I couldn't remember the last time I got some sleep this damn good.

"Stop staring at me you creep." she mumbled.

"Shut yo ass up." I said, pressing a kiss to her forehead.

She smiled, nestling closer. "You're such an ass."

"And you have a fat one." I said before slapping her ass cheek.

Her laughter was soft, and I couldn't help but join in.

———

Later that day, we joined the family for lunch. The family home was as lively as ever, with everyone crowded around the dining table.

"Well look what the wind blew in." Zeke teased as we walked in.

"Late as hell and we hungry as hell! Xander added, making everyone laugh.

Cassie blushed, but I wrapped an arm around her waist, holding her close. "Leave us alone. We were busy."

Kenzo raised an eyebrow. "Never thought I'd see the day Baby Bro. The way you used to clown us for being whipped. Now look at you."

"I just hadn't met the right woman. Sue me mufucka. Plus, Cassie is different." I admitted, shrugging.

"She better be. We don't let just anyone into this family." Pilar said jokingly, but I knew she was serious too.

Cassie smirked at her. "It wouldn't matter cuz I'm not going nowhere!"

"i know that's right!" Mama said making all the men smack their lips.

"What the hell you know about that woman?" Sayid asked playfully.

"Y'all are some haters!" Mama replied while pointing.

As the afternoon went on, I couldn't help but watch Cassie interact with everyone. She was laughing with Genesis, playing with Zahra, even helping Mama in the kitchen. This woman was fucking perfect and if any nigga thought they could take her from me, I hope they had nine lives.

That night, after we got home, Cassie and I sat on the couch with her head resting on my shoulder.

"Today was nice." she said softly.

"It was. I never thought I'd have this. A family, a future." I admitted.

"You have it now. And you better get used to it. Cuz you're not getting rid of us." she said, turning to look at me.

I smiled, leaning down to kiss her. "Good. Because I don't want to."

I can't believe I done turned into a simp like my brothers. This shit is wild. But... I fuck with it!

EPILOGUE

Cassie

I stood outside of my spa "Pure Essence Spa & Wellness", the sound of chatter from family, friends, and supporters filled the space. Balloons framed the front entrance, and danced in the breeze, and a bright red ribbon stretched across the doors. My nerves were high, but my chest was full of pride.

A year ago, I never would've imagined this moment. Standing here as a business owner, surrounded by love and support. I took a deep breath, gripping the microphone tightly as I stepped forward to address the crowd.

"Hey y'all!" I began.

"Thank you all for being here. This moment means more to me than I can put into words. Opening this spa has been a dream of mine for as long as I can remember, and seeing it come to life today is like a dream come true." I said.

The crowd cheered, and I smiled as my eyes scanned the familiar faces before me.

"First and foremost, I want to thank my girls—Genesis, Pilar, Phoenix, Rayne, and my cousin Shya." I gestured toward them, and they waved back, smiling.

"Each of you has played a huge role in getting this place up and running. From helping me decorate to keeping me sane on days when I felt like giving up. You've been my rock. I love you all more than words can say."

They all screamed that they loved me back, making everyone laugh.

I turned to the small group of employees standing nearby.

"To my new team... thank you for believing in me and trusting me to lead you. I'm so excited to start this journey with you."

My eyes landed on my mom, standing near the front. Her smile was so bright that she could light up a room.

"Mom, you've been my biggest cheerleader for my entire life. You showed me what it means to be a strong woman and an amazing mother. Every move I make is because of the foundation you gave me, and I just hope and pray that I'm making you proud."

My mom mouthed the words "I love you" and I returned the gesture.

Tears blurred my vision as I glanced toward the Drakos family.

"To my new family. Kenzo, Adonis, Xander, Zeke, Adara, and Sayid. You welcomed me and my daughter with open arms and showed us what unconditional support looks like. Thank you for everything you've done to make us feel like we belong."

All the men nodded, while Adara smiled widely and blew me a kiss.

I turned toward Carlie, who was perched on Jabari's neck, beaming at me with that beautiful smile I adored.

"Carlie, you are my reason why. Every move I make, every decision, is for you. You are the best daughter I could ever ask for, and the best thing that ever happened to me. I hope you know how much I love you."

"I love you too Mommy!" Her little voice said.

I then looked down at my man and had to prepare myself.

"And last but definitely not least...Jabari."

He locked eyes with me, and it was like everyone around us had disappeared.

"Jabari, you've changed my life in ways I never thought were possible. You've taught me what love is supposed to feel like. What it means to truly be loved and supported. You've been my partner, my protector, and my best friend. I wouldn't be standing here without you, and I can't thank you enough for everything you've done for me and Carlie. Even the shit that I didn't know about or consent to."

Everyone close to us laughed at that part including him.

"I say all this to say that I love you with all my heart." I concluded.

"I love you more Mama!" He shouted proudly.

The crowd erupted into applause, but all I could focus on was the way Jabari was looking at me. Whew that man!

EPILOGUE

Jabari

I didn't think it was possible to love Cassie more than I already did, but listening to her speech just now proved me wrong. She had this way of shining so bright that you couldn't help but be drawn to her.

As the crowd cheered and Cassie stepped forward to cut the ribbon, I slipped the small velvet box out of my pocket. My heart raced, but not because I was nervous. I was excited as hell. This was it.

She held the scissors high as the ribbon fell to the ground causing everyone to clap and cheer. Cassie turned toward me with a smile that filled her entire face. But then her eyes widened as she saw me drop to one knee.

Gasps rippled through the crowd, and everyone suddenly became quiet.

"Cassie..." I started.

"From the moment you came into my life, you turned everything upside down in the best possible way. You made me want to be a better man. Not just for you, but for

Carlie, too. You've shown me what love is supposed to look like, and I can't imagine spending another day of my life without you."

Her hand flew to her mouth with tears spilling down her cheeks as I opened the box to reveal the ring.

"I was a player, Cassie. A fucking Mack! I'm talking a different woman every…"

"Okay nigga! I get it!" She snapped, making everyone laugh.

"My bad! Anyways, I was a man who thought he'd never settle down. But then I met you, and I knew that I would do anything to have you. To keep you. I just wanted to make you and Carlie happy. I want to build a life with you. And if you let me, I will make you the happiest woman alive. Will you marry me?" I asked.

Cassie began sobbing as she nodded frantically before throwing herself into my arms. "Yes! Of course! I would love to marry you!"

The crowd erupted into cheers and applause as I pulled her into my arms.

Ya boy is getting married!

I watched her walk around the spa laughing and chatting with everyone. I caught her staring at her ring a few times and felt proud. I asked her to describe her perfect ring for me one day and went and got it custom made. It felt good to know that she loved it. I better get unlimited head and pussy for that mufucka for life. That bitch set me back a nice ass chunk!

As I stood there chatting with my brothers, I had to

laugh to myself. My playboy days are over. I'd finally met my fucking match!

And I wouldn't have it any other way.

THE END!

SPECIAL THANKS

Thank you for reading my latest release, The Brotherhood of The Drakos Mafia Part 3! I truly hope you all enjoyed it! I have so much more in store for you all and I appreciate you sticking it out with me! It's been a rough year for me and the support that I still receive means the world to me! Please, if you have time, leave an honest review on Amazon for me! I would love to hear your thoughts and opinions on my work whether it's good or bad! For all updates and information on book releases, add and follow my pages below! I hope you enjoyed it!
IG: destiny_amor
FB: https://bit.ly/3iGIOC5
Amazon: https://amzn.to/3Wc3FuQ
Catalog Links: https://linktr.ee/desamor

TEXT ALERTS

If you want exclusive priority updates and info on all releases and material, click the link below and subscribe for text and email alerts! You can also text "desamor" to 855-931-3238!

Text Alerts: https://slktxt.io/ZKfr

DES'AMOR CATALOG

Mesmerized By A Brew City Boss 1-3
Christmas With The Kys (A Holiday Novella)
Confessions of A BBL: A Bad B*tch Lifestyle 1-3
Deeply In Love With A Certified Billionaire 1-3
I Like 'Em Cocky & All About Me 1-3
I'm His Present & His Future (A Holiday Novella)
A Hood Love I Never Expected 1-3
The Brotherhood Of The Drakos Mafia 1-3

Made in the USA
Middletown, DE
28 August 2025

13160307R00116